If coolness could be rated on a 10-point scale, Richard would be at least a 9. He's one of the best basketball players at Westlake School, he's extremely good-looking, and his father is some big deal—not a mayor, but something like that.

When my hair's okay and I'm wearing something like the red sweater that zips and my black jeans, my looks might be about an 8, but today I wasn't wearing anything great and my hair is still a weird length because of the stupid haircut that made my ponytail about two inches long. I would have to say that in the copy room I looked 6.5, at best.

We're spending a lot of time studying inequalities in algebra now, which makes sense, since who you're greater than (>) and who you're less than (<) is kind of the point of eighth grade. So when I finished putting more paper in the top tray, I stepped aside and said, "Go ahead," because we both knew that Richard was > me (R>T).

⚬⚬⚬

ALSO BY WENDY LICHTMAN

Do The Math: The Writing on the Wall

Do the Math

Secrets, Lies, and Algebra

by Wendy Lichtman

Greenwillow Books
An Imprint of HarperCollinsPublishers

HarperTeen is an imprint of HarperCollins Publishers.

Do the Math: Secrets, Lies, and Algebra
Copyright © 2007 by Wendy Lichtman
All rights reserved. Printed in the United States of America.
No part of this book may be used or reproduced in any manner whatsoever without written permission except in the case of brief quotations embodied in critical articles and reviews. For information address HarperCollins Children's Books, a division of HarperCollins Publishers, 1350 Avenue of the Americas, New York, NY 10019.
www.harperteen.com

Library of Congress Cataloging-in-Publication Data
Lichtman, Wendy.
Do the math: secrets, lies, and algebra / by Wendy Lichtman.
"Greenwillow Books."
p. cm.
Summary: Tess has always loved math, and she uses mathematical concepts to help her understand things in her life, so she is dismayed to find out how much math—and life—can change in eighth grade.
ISBN 978-0-06-122955-8 (trade bdg.)
ISBN 978-0-06-122956-5 (lib. bdg.)
ISBN 978-0-06-122957-2 (pbk.)
[1. Mathematics—Fiction. 2. Honesty—Fiction. 3. Middle schools—Fiction. 4. Schools—Fiction. 5. Friendship—Fiction.] I. Title.
PZ7.L6Do 2007 [Fic]—dc22 2006033712

Typography by Victoria Jamieson
❖
First HarperTeen paperback edition, 2008

To Camsie Matis, a remarkable teacher
who loves both mathematics and the children
with whom she works

And to Charleen Calvert,
a brilliant principal who nurtures
quality teaching like Camsie's in the public schools

Chapter 1   Inequalities   1

Chapter 2   Graphs   6

Chapter 3   Tangents   15

Chapter 4   DNE   24

Chapter 5   Circular Thinking   32

Chapter 6 ·   Venn Diagrams   39

Chapter 7   The Difference Between
               Axioms and Theorems   52

Chapter 8   Zero   61

Chapter 9   Percentages   71

Chapter 10   The Quadratic Equation   75

Chapter 11   Parallel Lines   81

Chapter 12   A Complete Circle   90

Chapter 13	The Number Line	94
Chapter 14	Prime Numbers	100
Chapter 15	One More DNE	109
Chapter 16	Imaginary Numbers	119
Chapter 17	The Additive Property of Equality	128
Chapter 18	Extraneous Solutions	140
Chapter 19	Asymptotes, Non-Euclidean Geometry, and Other Things I Didn't Learn Yet	153
Chapter 20	Lines and Line Segments	162
Chapter 21	Exponents	174
Chapter 22	Infinity	179

Chapter 1

Inequalities

The copy room at my school is actually just a closet next to Ms. Balford's office, so when Richard came in and said, "Hey, Tess," he was standing about two inches behind me. "Could I borrow the machine for a second?" he whispered, closing the door quietly.

I took a stack of paper from the drawer, turned away from Richard, and refilled the empty tray while I tried to decide what I should answer.

The only reason I'm allowed to use the copy machine is that it's my job to make three hundred copies of the newsletter every Thursday. Ms. Balford never exactly said that I shouldn't let anyone else in the room, but when she showed me where she hung the key she made a big deal about how she trusted me, so I knew I wasn't supposed to let anyone just stroll in.

"I heard you were the reason the math team won on Saturday," Richard said before I decided anything.

"Not really," I said, but I kind of smiled at that, because in the final round I was the one who had answered the last question correctly, so in a way it was true that I was the reason we won.

If coolness could be rated on a 10-point scale, Richard would be at least a 9. He's one of the best basketball players at Westlake School, he's extremely good-looking, and his father is some big deal—not a mayor, but something like that.

On basketball game days the boys on the team have to wear ties to school, so that afternoon in the copy room Richard was wearing a light blue shirt with a green and blue tie that had a small print of Mickey Mouse on it. It may not sound great, but he looked very good.

When my hair's okay and I'm wearing something like the red sweater that zips and my black jeans, my looks might be about an 8, but today I wasn't wearing anything great and my hair is still a weird length because of the stupid haircut that made my ponytail about two inches long. Miranda says I have "naturally great skin" because I don't break out, and "perfect proportions" because I'm not skinny or fat, but even Miranda says the haircut was a mistake. Anyway, I would have to say that in the copy room I looked 6.5, at best.

We're spending a lot of time studying inequalities in algebra now, which makes sense, since who you're greater than (>) and who you're less than (<) is kind of the point of eighth grade. So when I finished putting more paper in the top tray, I stepped aside and said, "Go ahead," because we both knew that Richard was > me (R>T).

Richard acted like he wasn't doing anything wrong, but I could tell that he was trying to hide the papers he was copying. I pretended to look for the stapler so he wouldn't think I was snooping, but Richard is not stupid.

Neither am I. When I saw the words "Your Constitution" and about five pages of questions, I knew exactly what he was doing. Next Monday all eighth graders have to take a test on the U.S. Constitution, and Richard had obviously stolen the test off Mr. Wright's desk and was making a copy so he could put the original one back and not get caught.

Richard has these perfectly straight teeth even though he never wore braces, and you can tell he knows how good he looks when he smiles. He smiled at me when he finished copying the stolen test and said, "Thanks a lot, Tess," and I said, "No problem," even though there was one.

The problem was that I felt angry because Richard thought he could sneak into the copy room when I was in there and I wouldn't say anything because of who he is. I was angry at myself, too, because I *didn't* say anything. And I know that if someone like Lynn, who lies all the time and tells everyone that she's best friends with Miranda and me, had come in to copy a stolen test when I was working, I would have told her no way, because it's pretty obvious that L<T.

In math, if a number is greater than or less than another one, that never changes. The inequality 11>7 is always true, for example. But with people, that's not the way it works.

Now that I know Richard stole the U.S. Constitution test, and he knows I know, I think our inequality may have changed. Maybe now T ≥ R.

Chapter 2

Graphs

I was surprised to hear my mother talking on the phone when I walked into the house after school, because she usually teaches late on Thursdays. I knew she was speaking to my dad when I heard her ask, "Will you be home soon?" in a voice that sounded like she was trying not to cry, and I guess I knew it was something I wasn't exactly supposed to hear, because I stopped walking so I wouldn't make any noise. Mom was standing in the kitchen facing the back window, and I was in the hallway where she could have seen me if she'd turned around, so it's not like I was really hiding.

"It seems like it was a suicide," my mother said. "Rob says Nina locked herself in their car in the garage, turned on the engine, and sat there until the carbon monoxide poisoned her." My mother's voice was shaking when she said, "But I don't think so."

Even though I was standing perfectly still, I could feel my heart start to pound. Rob was my mother's friend who taught sculpting at Art4Kids, where she taught ceramics. I knew he was sort of famous, because I'd seen his work at the Oakland Museum of Art. Nina was his wife.

I leaned a little bit to the left so I could see my mother's reflection in the window. She was looking down at the floor, and the hand that wasn't holding the phone was covering her eyes. It was hard for me to understand her, but I was nearly positive she said, "I think Rob was involved."

That's impossible, I thought, taking a couple of quiet steps closer. Because if I heard her right, it meant that my mother was saying that Nina didn't really commit suicide but that Rob had *killed* her.

My mother hung up the phone, pulled out a chair, and sat down at the kitchen table. Her eyes were wide open and she was staring at absolutely nothing, which made her look like some cartoon character who couldn't believe what had just happened. Except if she were a cartoon, she would have had exclamation points and question marks all around her head, which might seem funny, but in real life when you see your mother looking like that, you get scared.

"Mom?" I asked quietly, and waited a couple seconds for her to answer.

"*Mom,*" I said louder, trying to get her to snap out of it.

My mother blinked her eyes and turned toward me. "Hi, honey," she said in what was supposed to be a normal voice.

"Are you okay?" I asked.

Mom turned away and looked like she was going to go back into her zombie state.

"Did you go to the studio this morning?" I asked. Rob has a large studio, with a kiln, in a building behind his house. My mother rents space there so she has a place to work on her own projects, like these ceramic frames she's making now.

"I did," my mother said, staring straight ahead again. "Nina's dead," she said sadly.

I sat down in my father's place at the table and spoke quietly. "And you think Rob might have done it?" I asked.

My mom shook her head.

"Mom," I said, nearly whispering. "I was standing right here. I heard you."

Mom looked directly at me. "I can't talk now, Tess," she said. "Why don't you go upstairs and start your homework?"

"Can I just ask you one more question?"

"Not now," she said, standing up and walking out of the kitchen.

That's not right, I thought. Even if you're in shock and really upset, you still shouldn't let me think Rob might have killed Nina and then not answer one more question.

Actually, I had about a hundred more questions. As I walked upstairs to my bedroom, I wanted to know how, exactly, Nina had died, and I wanted to know why my mother even *thought* that Rob was involved. I wondered if carbon monoxide takes a long time or just a second to poison you, and I wondered if my mother believed that Rob had killed Nina in some other way and then put her body in the car.

When I got to my room, I dropped my backpack on the floor, threw my jacket on the bed, and pictured Rob. Miranda and I had taken his Hands in Clay class last summer, and on the first day he'd given us each a huge lump of clay and said, "Your job is to find what's in there that wants to come out." No matter what you made, Rob always had something positive to say about your work.

The only time I'd ever met Nina was at their holiday party—she was wearing a dark purple dress, and I think she was a lot older than Rob because her hair was gray. She asked me if I wanted to use the computer in her office, which was very nice of her because I was the only kid there and she could see I was bored.

Sitting on the floor of my room, leaning back against my bed, I could feel that I was sort of shaking. There was no way I was going to do any homework, so I don't know why I unzipped my backpack and dumped out all my books.

"Graph something that's meaningful to you," Ms. Saltzman had told us when she'd said the homework was to plot a "real-life graph." Even though I knew I'd never hand it in, I tore off a sheet of graph paper and tried to draw Nina's death.

If she just breathed in the carbon monoxide, fell asleep, and never woke up, then I thought that the graph would dip slowly in a soft arc, like the one we drew of aluminum foil cooling. If point A is alive and point D is dead, then Nina started at the top of the y-axis, wide-awake at (0, 20). The garage door was closed, the motor was on, maybe she was even listening to music as she got dizzy and fell asleep. Little by little her breathing got slower until, at the coordinates of, say, (18, 0), she was dead.

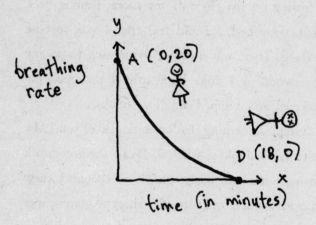

But if Nina just took a whiff of the stuff and died, then the graph would clunk right down to the bottom of the y-axis, taking no time at all, like the graph we made of a book dropping.

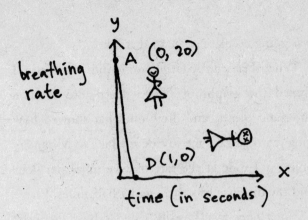

If Rob killed Nina some other way and put her body in the car, then there wouldn't be any graph at all, because Nina would be dead from the very beginning. Or maybe he put something like a sleeping pill in her food, then carried her into the car after she was asleep, turned on the motor, and snuck out of there.

But I didn't even try to draw that, because if you know Rob, that seems completely impossible. Rob is not a sneaky person. He's an extremely nice person— like when I made this lousy sculpture of a girl on a bike, Rob said, "You've got some fine movement there," even though anybody could see that that girl was going no place at all on that bike.

When I heard my father come into the house, I ripped the graphs of Nina's death into about a thousand pieces, and drew one that showed how long it would take me to ride my bike to Miranda's house if I rode at the rate of five miles per hour and the distance was three and a half miles. I have no idea how fast I really ride or how far away Miranda's house really is, but everyone knows that's the kind of thing you're supposed to be graphing in eighth grade.

Chapter 3
Tangents

Usually, right after my father comes home from work, my mother calls me for dinner, but about twenty minutes passed and still nobody had called my name. I knew my parents were talking about Rob and Nina, so before they decided to leave me out completely, I went downstairs.

When I came into the kitchen, my father was leaning against the counter, looking at the floor. "Hi, honey," he said, without looking up. Then he shook his head sadly and sat down. I sat too, but even though all the food was on the table, Mom stayed standing behind her chair, and for more than a minute none of us moved.

When my mother finally said, "I kept feeling that Rob was trying to distract me from something," Dad put his napkin on his lap, and I looked from him to Mom, feeling really relieved that they were going to let me listen.

My mother kept standing while she told us the details of Nina's death.

Early that morning my mother had forgotten her keys to Rob's studio, so when she got there she walked around to the front of his house to ring the bell.

"Nina's gone," Rob had said when he'd opened the door. "She's *gone*," he'd whispered.

Mom had thought he'd meant that Nina had moved out because, like she said as she sat down, "It wouldn't be the first time Rob and Nina decided they couldn't live together."

But that's not what Rob had meant by "gone."

While my mother had sat with him waiting for the police to come, and dead Nina had sat in the car in the cold, closed garage, Rob told Mom that he had known something was wrong as soon as he woke up that morning because Nina's side of the bed was empty and the cat was on her pillow. Then he'd thought for a minute and said, "No, no, what am I saying? The cat is out there dead with her. Of course it wasn't in bed with me. Nina took the cat with her. She took it everywhere. One time when we drove to Toronto she took the cat, and we were staying in a fine hotel. Oh, I'll never go to Toronto with Nina again," Rob had said. And then he'd cried.

"It was things like that," Mom told us, "that started giving me the creeps. Rob would say something, then catch himself and go off on some strange tangent."

In math a tangent is a straight line that touches the circumference of a circle at one point. So if the truth of how Nina died was in that circle, then maybe at any point that Rob felt he touched the circle, he headed off on a tangent to get as far away as he could from the real story.

"This is awful," my father said, shaking his head. My parents were both speaking in very low voices, even though there was nobody in the house but the three of us. "What would he gain from her death?" my father asked, so quietly I could hardly hear him.

"Well," Mom whispered, "money, for one thing. Nina was a very rich woman."

Dad passed the chicken, Mom passed the potatoes,

and I waited a few more minutes before I asked, "What else was creepy?"

My mother shrugged. "He was just rambling on and on, and every once in a while he'd say something I couldn't believe I heard right."

"Like?" Dad asked.

Mom unfolded her napkin before she answered. "Like Rob told me that when he saw Nina searching for her knit slippers, he wondered why she cared if her feet were cold when she was about to die anyway." My mother shuddered like she was freezing cold herself even though it was warm in our house, and my father swallowed hard even though he hadn't eaten anything yet.

"So either," Dad whispered, "it was suicide and he knew about it and didn't try to stop her, or . . ." Dad stopped and shook his head.

"Or it wasn't," I said.

"Right after Rob heard himself say that," Mom said, "he launched into this whole story about the woman who had knit the slippers—that her name was Sarah, and that she was nearly blind and couldn't see what she was knitting. He said that didn't stop her, though, that she was fast and accurate and it was remarkable to watch her knit. I swear he must have talked about this blind woman's knitting for ten minutes.

"I know Rob was distraught," my mother said, "but when he blabbered on like that, I really felt that he was trying to distract me from something."

My mother looked at the food on her plate and said, "When the police arrived, Rob had had time to think about it some more. So he told them that Nina had had a tragic childhood and was very depressed and had refused to get help. By then," Mom said, "there was no mention of cats or slippers."

Even though nobody else could possibly hear us, my voice was very quiet too when I asked my mother if she'd talked to the police yet.

"I don't think it's my place to do that," she answered, and then, in a normal voice, not the secret-telling tone, my mother said, "Pass the salt, please."

"But if you really think he might have *murdered* her," I said.

"Mom doesn't have real evidence, Tess," my father interrupted.

"She just *told* us evidence," I said.

"No," my father insisted, "she just told us she has a bad feeling, and you can't accuse someone of murder because you have a bad feeling."

"Exactly," my mother agreed, opening her eyes wide and sort of twitching her head in my direction, which is the little secret code my parents have that means *Don't talk about it anymore in front of Tess.* Then Mom turned to me and said, "Please, Tess, *please* don't say a word about this to anyone."

"I won't," I said. "I promise."

"We'd like you to keep this completely private," my father said, even though I'd just promised I would. "We don't want to start any rumors."

"I know, Dad."

My mother picked up her fork and squished some butter into her baked potato, and when I asked, "But you believe he did it, don't you, Mom?" she took a little more butter and squished again. "I believe he may have," she finally admitted, "but Rob's wife had just died, and if there's ever a time when you can be expected to be confused, it's when your wife has just died. I would never go to the police based only on his confusion."

Sometimes your opinion of things can change in about two seconds. Before, I'd always thought my parents were the kind of people who tried to do what was right, but not telling the police when you know about a possible murder is definitely not right.

Two seconds earlier I'd thought that my favorite

dinner was barbeque chicken and baked potato, but as I looked at my plate, I didn't even want to taste it.

"May I have the sour cream?" my father asked.

"I'm trying to use all organic dairy products now," my mother said.

"Good," my father agreed. "It's better for us and it's better for the cows."

I looked from my mother, who was busy shaking salt onto her potato, to my father, who was dropping huge globs of organic sour cream onto his, and I thought: *Talk about going off on a tangent. My mother's friend may have just killed his wife and my parents are sitting there talking about cows.*

Chapter 4

ONE

The next morning in algebra class, while I was supposed to be thinking about the problems on page 265, I was actually wondering how you'd report a murder if you wanted to. I thought it would probably be wrong to call 911, because that's for emergencies, and it's not exactly an emergency after the police already have been to the house and taken the dead person's body to the morgue.

To report that kind of murder—the kind that

looks like it was a suicide—I think you should probably go to a police station and ask to speak to a homicide detective. But maybe you need an adult to go with you—maybe there's some law that says you have to be eighteen or twenty-one to report a possible murder although, in my opinion, that wouldn't be right.

"When you finish problems one through seven," Ms. Saltzman said, opening her stamp pad, "please raise your hand so I can check your work."

Even though I didn't raise my hand, Ms. Saltzman came past my desk and stamped the top of my paper. "You know what that's called, Tess?" she asked me, pointing to the hexagonal designs her stamp had made.

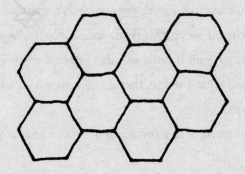

I turned my head and turned my paper, then said, "Beehive?"

"The real term is *tessellation*," Ms. Saltzman said, "which is a pattern that's formed when you cover a surface with congruent shapes. And yes, a beehive is a tessellation."

"*Tess*ellation," I repeated. "I like that."

"I thought you would." Then Ms. Saltzman smiled and continued going around the room stamping people's work with a cool design that sounds like my name.

Ms. Saltzman is my favorite teacher, but I still wouldn't ask her to come with me to the police station. It would probably be against the school rules for her to do something like that anyway, and I'm sure she'd have to talk to my parents first.

In the back of my algebra notebook, there's a section where I write my private ideas. I do it in sort of a code, so even if someone disrespected my privacy and read what I wrote, they'd still have no idea what it meant.

The code I use for Sammy is s^5, because she's

always so much drama. She exaggerates everything as if it were raised to at least the fifth power. When a number has an exponent, it means that you have to multiply the number by itself that many times, so even if the number is small—say three—it can get big quickly: 3^5=3x3x3x3x3=243. Sometimes Sammy even answers a question five times. I'm not kidding. When I asked her if she thought Damien was cute, she said, "Yes, yes, yes, yes, yes!" So, even though she's one of my best friends, I wouldn't tell Sammy about my mother's secret, because she'd get way too dramatic.

I also wouldn't tell Miranda, even though she knows Rob and has been my closest friend all through middle school. The code I use for Miranda is the absolute value sign, $|m|$, because with absolute value, there are no negatives—absolute value only tells how far away a number is from zero on the number line. So since −7 and +7 are both 7 spaces away from zero, $|-7|$=7, which is an example of how negative numbers become positive. That's exactly like Miranda, who is the most positive person I know. Even if you tell her you've done something totally stupid, she makes you feel like you didn't really do anything wrong, which is usually a great quality for a friend to have.

But the reason I don't want to tell Miranda that my mother isn't reporting her killer friend is that Miranda might come up with a reason my *mother* isn't doing anything wrong. That's the problem with people who are totally positive.

I looked at the s^5 and $|m|$ I'd written on the back of my paper. *I can't tell them anyway,* I thought, erasing both symbols. *I can't tell anyone.*

I don't have a symbol for myself, so I just use my initial, T, which means nothing, of course. If I ever think of a symbol that expresses something important about me, I'm going to draw it on the inside of my ankle, on the soft spot right below the bone. I once saw a girl with a tattoo of a butterfly there, and I really liked the way it looked.

"Okay," Ms. Saltzman said as she wrote y=2x-1 and

y-2x=3 on the board, "let's see if you can solve this one."

After four people (including me) gave wrong answers, Ms. Saltzman finally admitted that there were *no* numbers for x and y that would satisfy both equations. "What we have here, folks, is a problem without a solution. When you come across problems that can't be solved," she said, "you may write DNE, which means Does Not Exist. The answer to this problem does not exist."

"All *right*," Marcus said, like he'd been looking for an answer like DNE his whole life. You could just tell that from now on half the answers on Marcus's tests would say "DNE."

But I felt the opposite. While Ms. Saltzman blabbed on about how we'd be learning the formula for identical slopes, which would explain why these equations had no point in common and therefore no solution, I felt annoyed.

It might sound strange, but the two things I used to trust most of all were my mother and math.

Mom, because she was the kind of person who, if

she told you something, you knew it was true, and even if you were young, she didn't act like you wouldn't understand.

And math, because it was the place where something was either right or wrong, and where there was an answer to every problem.

But now, I thought as I scribbled the stupid letters D, N, and E in my notebook, my mother's acting like she doesn't even want to know the truth, and now there are "solutions" that Do Not Exist.

I was one of the last people to leave the room when the bell rang, and Damien was too, which made me feel like he was waiting for me. Damien is only a little taller than me, which I like because when I talk to him I don't need to look up. When we walk next to each other, it feels like we're good friends, even though we don't really know each other outside of algebra, which is the only class we have together.

"What's wrong?" Damien asked when we got into the hall.

"I think DNE is stupid," I said.

"I suppose," he said, and laughed a little before he turned to go upstairs to the science room.

The halls at Westlake are extremely crowded when we change classes, and even though the teachers stand outside their doorways to keep us from fooling around, Richard managed to bump into me when I walked past him. Then he smiled his really good smile and said, "Hey, Tess."

Chapter 5
Circular Thinking

The very first thing that Mr. Wright talked about in history class was the U.S. Constitution test. "This test is of infinite importance" is what he said, which is, of course, ridiculous. *Infinite* means that there's no end to something—that it's immeasurable. You can never get to the end of the number line, for example, because you can always add one more number, so that *is* infinite. But give me a break, no test is close to being of "infinite importance."

Mr. Wright is always making mistakes like that

when he says anything that has to do with math. I know he's not a complete idiot, though, because he's actually very good at teaching history.

I sort of glanced over at Richard, who sits in front of me to the right, and watched him zip his back-pack, then unzip it, then zip it again while Mr. Wright talked about the infinitely important test.

"I apologize, class," Mr. Wright said, "for telling you there would be three essay questions. I received the exams from the state yesterday, and I see that it is, in fact, all multiple choice. I'm afraid I'm going to have to do a complete three-sixty on this."

This is another perfect example of how hard math is for Mr. Wright. A circle has 360 degrees, so when you do a "complete 360" you go all the way around and end up at the very same place you started— which would mean that the test would *still* have three essay questions.

essay questions   multiple choice

What Mr. Wright meant to say was that he was doing a 180, which would take him halfway around the circle; that way he would come out on the other side to all multiple choice.

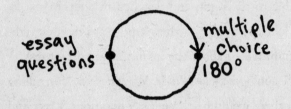

I raised my hand at the exact same time Mr. Wright was asking who would volunteer to pass out the study guide for the exam, so when he said "Tess," and I said, "It's only one hundred and eighty degrees," he squinted at me like I was something too close for him to read without glasses. "Well, thank you," he said as he handed me the pile of papers.

Richard obviously didn't need a study guide, so I walked right past him, but when he looked up and put out his hand, I dropped one on his desk, and he said, "*Gracias.*" Luis, who sits next to him, kind of laughed at that, but even if I didn't know Richard was a thief and a cheater, I wouldn't think there was anything funny about saying "thank you" in Spanish. Even if Richard were still > me, I don't think I would have laughed.

As soon as I gave Luis his study guide, he took off the top of the thin black pen he always uses and began drawing in the margins. Luis will draw on anything: he's got a lion growling on one of his sneakers and two tiny cars racing each other down the inside of his left arm. Whenever you see a fake tattoo that's really good, you know that Luis was the artist.

I can make 3-D letters that look good, but other than that, I'm not an artist at all, even though you might think I would be because of my mom. Miranda's in charge of the decorating committee for the winter dance, and she asked me to make a banner that says "Celebrate!" for the wall of the cafeteria, which is the only kind of thing I can draw.

"The Bill of Rights!" Mr. Wright announced, rubbing his hands together like he was about to eat the most delicious dessert. "Ah! The Bill of Rights!" he repeated as I put the extra study guides on his desk and sat down. "Sammy, can you tell us exactly what the Bill of Rights is?"

Whenever Mr. Wright wants the right answer quickly, he calls on Sammy, and really, you can't blame him, because why take an hour to get an answer that she can give you in one second?

"The first ten amendments to the Constitution," Sammy answered in exactly one second.

Mr. Wright nodded and looked around the room. "And an example?" he asked.

Lynn said freedom of speech, which is the one amendment we all know since Mr. Wright has been talking about it since the first day of school.

"Thank you, Lynn, for starting us with the First Amendment," Mr. Wright said. "Others?" he asked.

After people started giving all these made-up freedoms, like the freedom to wear the kind of clothes you like and the freedom to chew gum in school, Sammy said something real. She said that the Sixth Amendment said you had the right to a speedy trial, and the right to know who witnessed the crime, and the right to a defense lawyer.

"Is your hand up, Richard?" Mr. Wright asked, and Richard looked directly at me when he said, "Freedom to privacy."

"Hm," Mr. Wright said. "Say more, please."

"Privacy," Richard said. "Like it's nobody's business what you're doing."

Mr. Wright is a very nice person, so he always tries to make the answer sound right even if it's way off. "I think you might be referring to the Fourth Amendment," Mr. Wright said to Richard. "That is unnecessary search and seizure, which means that the police can't search you or your home without probable cause; they can't look in your house without first getting a search warrant from the court. Is that what you're speaking about?" he asked Richard.

"Yeah," Richard said, but I knew that wasn't true. I knew that Richard was really talking about the freedom to steal a test and not get caught.

Mr. Wright doesn't usually say three stupid math things in one day, but today he outdid himself. When he divided us into groups to talk about what we'd want in the Westlake Bill of Rights, he pointed to Marcus, Richard, and James, and said, "Okay, you three are a pair."

It's impossible for three of anything to be a pair. It's like saying, "Okay, you three are a dozen." But Mr. Wright just kept going around the room pointing to threesomes and saying, "Okay, you three by the window—you're a pair."

There are thirty-three kids in the class, so Mr. Wright must have said that very same stupid thing eleven times.

Chapter 6

Venn Diagrams

I was sitting on the bed in Miranda's room Saturday morning, picking little fuzz balls off a white turtleneck sweater she said she wanted to give away, when I looked up and noticed the clay head she had made in Rob's class last summer. It's a sculpture of a smiling girl, and the great thing about it is that it's not just the girl's mouth that's smiling, but her whole face—her cheekbones are raised and her eyes are crinkled, and there's even a small dimple in one cheek. The way you can tell that Miranda's an excellent artist is that when you look at that clay girl, you feel like smiling back.

But Saturday morning I didn't feel like smiling back, because when I looked at that girl, I thought of Rob. I wondered how he did it—if he did it—and I felt bad that my mother had no morals.

"I wish I could get rid of my clothes and get all new ones," Miranda told Sammy and me. Then she sat on the floor, opened the bottom drawer of her dresser, and asked us if we could keep a secret. When we both said, "Of course," Miranda told us that she had kissed James a few times and dreamed of him twice.

"I predicted that!" Sammy said. "I told you last *year* that he liked you!" Sammy kind of sung out, "Ooh, ooh, you guys are gonna get married," then punched her fist into the air and said, "Yeah, yeah, yeah, yeah, yeah!"

One of the other codes in the back of my math notebook is that sometimes I draw Venn diagrams about me and other people. I draw a circle that represents someone and a circle that represents me, and where the two circles intersect is where we're alike. In all other ways, we're different.

In the Venn diagram of Miranda and me, there's a lot of meaningless stuff in our intersection (same grade, both girls, same height, both lefties). But what makes me sad is that the really important things about us aren't in that shared area. Like I don't have any sisters or brothers, and Miranda has two brothers; I live with both my parents, but Miranda's father lives in Chicago. Also, she's very artistic, and she hates math. And now Miranda's kissed James, and I've kissed nobody.

(shaded area
represents
similarities)

"You and James are good together," I said, trying to make it sound like I was happy for her. "He's one of the nicest boys in the whole eighth grade."

"He really is," Miranda agreed.

"My next prediction," Sammy declared, pointing a finger at me, "is Tess and Damien. Oh, yes!" Then she turned to Miranda and asked if James had good lips and Miranda told her to please shut up, which was fine with me. I could see Sammy's reflection in the mirror, so I knew she didn't like it one bit that Miranda had told her to shut up. But she did shut up, and so did Miranda, and so did I for a while.

"These clothes are all from the beginning of middle school," Miranda said, tossing a cotton print skirt on the bed. "I want to wear something shiny and long to the dance," she said, taking a pair of old brown sandals from the back of her closet. "And I want high heels. I want clothes that fit who I am *now*."

My dress for the winter dance is black, even though the day my mom and I went shopping, she kept telling me how much better I looked in bright colors and hanging all these pink things in the dressing room for me to try on. Every time I stepped out of the dressing room in a light-colored dress, my mother gave me a thumbs-up sign, and every time I tried on a black one she said something like, "No, that's no good," or "That is just not appropriate for a middle school dance."

When I showed her this soft black dress with a zigzag hem, I could see that Mom tried to put her thumb down, but it just popped up like she couldn't control it. We both started laughing like maniacs then, so what could she do but let me get the dress?

I still think the dress is cool, but now it seems like it might be a little weird to wear a black dress with a zigzag hem to the school cafeteria. Truthfully, right now I don't care very much about the dress or the dance.

Just before I tried on the white fuzz-balled sweater, I looked at the smiling girl sculpture again, and in the two seconds it took me to pull the sweater over my head, I decided to tell the secret. Murder isn't the kind of thing you should keep from the police, I thought, and it isn't the kind of thing you should tell someone and make her promise to keep "completely private." It's too big for that.

"I've got a secret, too," I said. "It's sort of a huge one." Then, while Miranda and Sammy waited, I yanked down the back of the sweater and pushed up the sleeves a little.

"My mother knows about a possible murder," I finally said, "and she's not telling the cops."

Miranda dropped a pair of jeans on the floor and Sammy turned away from the mirror. After I explained about Rob and his mistakes the morning Nina died, Sammy said, "You guys know a *murderer*!"

Miranda sat down next to me on the bed, shook her head, and whispered, "I can't believe it." Her head kept shaking back and forth, and even though she didn't say it out loud, I could see her head saying, "No way." I could feel her mind insisting that Rob wasn't guilty.

"I once read about a guy in Canada who murdered

a woman with a sharpened icicle," Sammy said. "He stabbed her in the heart and the icicle melted, so there was no weapon, then he put her body in the bathtub so it looked like she had drowned."

"I can't believe it," Miranda said again, completely ignoring Sammy.

"Or maybe he gave his wife some poisoned food," Sammy said, picking up the jeans Miranda had dropped and slipping them on. "And she put some leftovers in the cat's bowl, so they both died and then Rob had to put the cat out there with her. Do you think he could have done something like that?" Sammy asked as she zipped up Miranda's jeans.

"I don't know," I said.

"Your mother should definitely tell so the police can find out," Sammy said.

Miranda picked up the green hooded sweatshirt she was giving to me and shook her head again. "He's so totally *nice*," she said.

"If your mom doesn't want to talk to the cops," Sammy continued, "then maybe *you* should."

"Tess can't do that!" Miranda snapped.

"Well, *somebody* should," Sammy said, opening the closet door so she could see the mirror again.

"But what if your mother did tell," Miranda said, hugging her old green sweatshirt, "and they investigated and found out Rob had nothing to do with it? If that happened, everyone would still think of him as a potential killer, which would be awful. And also, you never know what the cops will do if they think you're a potential killer—you'd probably be on some suspect list for the rest of your life."

While I thought about what Miranda said, I took off her white turtleneck sweater and handed it to Sammy. "This would look better on you," I said, "because you have boobs."

"I hate my boobs," Sammy said. She stood up and walked back to the mirror. "I hate these, too," she said, smacking her hips with her open hands. "You can't have these huge curves if you want to be a dancer," she said. "My mother still has the perfect

46

dancer's body. I can't believe I have her genes at all—we're completely different in every single way. Truthfully, I can't think of one thing my mother and I even *agree* on now," Sammy said as she turned around and looked over her shoulder to see her backside in the mirror. "I got this big stuff from my fat grandmother."

It's so obvious that Sammy's not fat that Miranda and I didn't even bother to say it.

"There was this Austrian emperor," Sammy said, "who killed the empress with a tiny thin blade and they never found out the cause because the hole was practically invisible." Sammy pulled on Miranda's sweater and took off the pink headband that was holding back her dark curls. "Maybe Rob did that and the police only think it's a suicide because the hole was invisible," she said.

Miranda completely ignored Sammy again, and just talked to me. "I think your mother should stay away from the whole thing, Tess—from Rob *and* from the cops," she said quietly. The inside of Miranda's eyes are so dark brown that they look nearly black, and I could see, looking into them, that she was scared. "If you really think Rob could be a murderer," she said, her dark eyes getting teary, "and if your mom goes to the cops, maybe he'll want to kill *her*. Maybe she's not telling because she's afraid of *that*."

"I really don't think so," I told Miranda. "I just think my mother's protecting Rob because he's her friend."

Sammy was looking at herself in Miranda's sweater which, with the black jeans and black boots she was wearing, looked extremely good on her. "I think your mother should tell," she said into the mirror, "but I know mine wouldn't."

The way Sammy spoke about her mother made me think of what Venn diagrams look like when the two sets have nothing in common—like, for example, the set of odd numbers and the set of even numbers. Their intersection is called an empty

set, because there's nothing in it. There's not one
number that can be both odd and even. I didn't like
thinking of Sammy and her mother like that—like
an empty set.

(no shaded
area at all)

And even though I didn't think my mother and I
were that way, I could sort of feel it coming. I could
feel our sets getting further apart, and I think that
was one reason I wanted Mom to tell the police
about Rob. Because if it were up to me, I knew I'd

tell, and if my mother wouldn't, well, that was one very big way we didn't intersect. That made us one step closer to becoming an empty set.

"Do you still want that sweatshirt?" I asked Miranda. "It's okay if you don't want to give it away."

"No, it's yours," Miranda said, handing it over. "I want to clean this place out." Then she looked at the clothes piled on the floor and said, "I just don't think Rob is like some Austrian emperor or a guy with an icicle."

Sammy sat down with us on the bed and shrugged. "I never met him," she admitted.

"You guys promise to keep this completely secret?" I asked.

Miranda and Sammy put their fists out and we all bumped knuckles, which means Yes, it's our secret and it's sealed.

It's possible for three sets to intersect, and I felt then that Miranda and Sammy and I did. Because sometimes you don't need to have the exact same things going on in your life to be connected to other people; sometimes you can intersect in really important ways just by telling each other your secrets.

(shaded area represents private things the three of us have told each other.)

Chapter 7
The Difference Between Axioms and Theorems

Here's a perfect example of why my code name for Sammy is s^5: when we were instant messaging last night and I asked her a simple question about talking to the cops, she blew it way out of proportion.

"Where do you think I should begin?" I typed.

"At the scene of the crime," she answered immediately.

"What do you mean?" I asked, even though I had a feeling I knew exactly what she meant. She meant the garage where Nina had died. What else could she mean?

Our computer is in a corner of the kitchen and both my parents were in the living room, which is only about ten feet away, so while I waited for Sammy to answer, I kept looking over my shoulder to make sure nobody showed up behind me. After five minutes Sammy still hadn't said anything, which probably meant she was messaging other people at the same time. "I don't think we should do this online," I wrote back. "Okay if I call you right now?"

"Yep," she answered, so I signed off and took the phone upstairs to my room.

"What does he look like?" Sammy asked the second she answered.

"Rob? Nothing special. Just a man. He has a short beard."

"Ah," Sammy said, like that meant something.

"Okay, here's what I think we should do," Sammy said. Then, before she could tell me, she yelled, "I'm just asking Tess about math homework, Mother. No, I'm not online. Yes, I know what you said—I'll be off in two minutes."

When Sammy came back to me, she said, "I think we should go to Rob's studio after school tomorrow. We'll pretend we're there to see your mother, but we'll really be doing our own investigation."

I'm not the sort of person who raises everything to the fifth power, so I had to explain to Sammy that I hadn't planned to do anything like that. "I want the *police* to do an investigation," I told her, "not us."

"But maybe you'll need to convince the police there's something to investigate," she said. "Maybe if we went there, we could come across some real evidence."

"Like what?" I asked.

"Like duct tape or plastic or something like that in the garage," Sammy said. "Because if she really did die from the poison gases, the garage had to have been sealed."

"That would only prove that she died in the garage," I said. "It wouldn't prove who did it. Anyway, I thought it was illegal to search someone's house without a warrant. I thought that was like

54

number five of the Bill of Rights."

"Number four," Sammy said. "But that's for the government anyway. *They* can't search without a warrant. Regular people can snoop as much as we want. It's not our fault if we stumble on some evidence that's in plain view."

"My mom won't even be working there tomorrow," I said. "She teaches at Art4Kids on Mondays."

"Listen," Sammy said, "I don't know why your mom's not telling the cops, but grown-ups cover for each other all the time. I think we should do *something* about this." Then she shouted, "I am *too* off the phone, Mother" and hung up.

I meant to study a little more for the Constitution test, but when I tried to read the Bill of Rights again, I could tell that my brain wasn't paying any attention. The only other homework I needed to do was my sustained silent reading, which meant twenty minutes of reading anything at all, so I took a book I'd already finished, went downstairs, and sat in the big tan chair. My father was lying on the couch reading a magazine, and my mother was sitting at the table paying bills.

"Mom," I said, after a few minutes, "can I ask you a question?"

My mother looked up and nodded.

"Can you tell me why you're not reporting Rob to the cops?"

"Your mother has no substantial proof, Tess," my father said, getting all protective, which is something he loves to do.

"*Mom?*" I said, meaning: I don't believe I heard anybody ask *you* a question, Dad.

"If the police are doing an investigation," my mother said, "they know where to find me. They took my name and phone number that morning."

"But maybe they aren't doing an investigation because they don't know there's something to investigate. Maybe you're the only one who knows anything."

"Honey, all I know is that Rob said a few strange things that made me feel uncomfortable. I am not about to accuse anyone of murder—this is *murder* we're talking about!—without substantial evidence." When my mother said the word *murder* she ripped an empty envelope in half. "I have not one shred of proof," she said, *rip, rip.*

"One more question," I said. "Do you know the difference between an axiom and a theorem?"

"Probably not," my father answered, even though, once again, I'm pretty sure nobody had asked *him* anything.

Whenever I used to interrupt my parents when I was a little kid, my father would hold up two fingers in my direction, which meant "Wait a couple minutes," and I was supposed to be quiet until those fingers were down. Holding up my own two fingers in Dad's direction, I said, "In math, if something is an *axiom,* it means you don't need proof for it to be true. Like, for example, when you multiply any number by one, that number is exactly the same as before you multiplied it, because it's an axiom that any number multiplied by one stays itself."

My mother was looking down at the bills, but she wasn't writing any checks or ripping any envelopes, so I was pretty sure she was listening. I glanced at Dad, lowered my fingers, and was a little surprised when he smiled and nodded.

"But for a *theorem*," I said, "you *do* need proof. You need to draw a line down the center of your page and explain what it is you're trying to prove and give step-by-step reasons. That's the only way you can know if a theorem is true or false."

Mom twisted her pen so the tip disappeared, then twisted it back out.

"In real life," I said, "I think it should be an axiom that if you know of a possible murder, you call the police. You don't need any proof to pick up the phone and call the cops."

"We can hear you just fine, Tess," my father said, which meant I was supposed to keep my voice down, and I almost gave him the "stay quiet" sign again.

"But before you *convict* someone of a crime," I said just as loudly, "you would need a huge proof—that's what a trial is! In court they'd have to start with the theorem 'Rob killed Nina,' and it would be up to the prosecutor—not you—to give the step-by-step proof, so they'd know if the theorem was true or false."

When my mother looked up at me, I lowered my voice. "Do you understand what I'm trying to say, Mom?" I asked more quietly.

"I do," my mother said. She put her pen down, folded her hands on the table, and said, "Tess, I have worked with Rob for about two years now, and I have never, ever seen him do anything hurtful—not to students, teachers, artists, anybody." My mother stared at her folded hands for a little while, then added, "I don't think Rob and his wife had a great marriage, and yes, I do have my suspicions because things sounded very strange that morning—but not strange enough to ruin a friend's life if he's not guilty." Then she picked up her pen again and said, "I understand your feelings, though."

No, you don't, I thought, closing the book I was

supposedly reading and walking into the kitchen. *You don't understand my feelings anymore, and you probably don't understand the difference between an axiom and a theorem, either. Because if you did, you'd call the cops.*

When I sat down at the computer again, I saw that Sammy was back online.

"Okay," I wrote. "Tomorrow, after school."

"Yes, yes, yes, yes, yes!" she answered.

Chapter 8
Zero

Mr. Wright scheduled a double period for us to take the U.S. Constitution test, which made it seem like maybe it *was* of infinite importance. The whole time I took it (from 9:17–11:02), I was thinking about going to Rob's studio after school.

"I have these rules," Sammy said when we were finally on the bus, "about when you should tell on someone, and this situation is definitely one of those times that I think it's required."

"What are your rules?" I asked.

Sammy dropped her backpack on the floor by our feet and turned in her seat to lean against the bus window. "If it's just property," she said, "like if I saw someone break into a locker, I'd never report it."

"Okay."

"But if somebody got hurt, or could get hurt, then yes, I'd tell."

"What about when you see someone cheating?" I asked, thinking that Richard probably got some fabulous grade on the test this morning. "Would you tell the teacher if you knew someone had cheated?"

"No way," Sammy said. "I wouldn't tell the teacher or anyone else, either. Because the cheater would trace it back to me—it always gets traced back to the original tattler—and I just don't want that kind of grief over someone else's grade. I pay attention to my own grades, that's all."

I was picking the cuticle of my thumbnail, which is this nervous thing I sometimes do, when Sammy leaned toward me and whispered, "Do you think Rob could be dangerous?" Actually, she didn't even whisper, she sort of mouthed the words, but I understood her perfectly.

I shook my head. "Not at all. There's no reason he'd suspect *us* of anything," I said. "We're kids. Also," I said, pulling a little chunk of skin from my thumb, "he seems like a nice guy."

Sammy nodded. "The history of the world is filled with nice guys who wouldn't hurt anyone else, except they kill their wives."

"Like who?" I asked.

"Henry the Eighth," Sammy said. "He chopped off his wife's head because he wanted to marry someone else."

We were passing the flower stand on College Avenue that's near Rob's house, but before I stood up, I leaned closer to Sammy. "One more thing," I whispered. "Nina had a lot of money."

"Motive number one," Sammy said, grabbing her backpack.

Even though Miranda and I went to Rob's studio every day last summer, I led Sammy the wrong way

63

on Oak Grove when we got off the bus. "Maybe we should have brought Miranda," I said, looking up and down the street for the right house.

"No, two people are better than three for an investigation," Sammy said as we walked back in the other direction. "Also, Miranda has soccer today."

"Okay, this one," I finally said, pointing to a big gray house with purple flowers growing up one corner. On each of the steps leading to the front door were little clay elves that I guess Rob, or maybe one of his students, had made. One of the elves sort of welcomed you in by pointing to the house and giggling, and another one was clapping its tiny hands like it was happy you'd come. I'd never seen them before, and if I hadn't been there to investigate a possible murder, I would have thought they were extremely cute.

"So this driveway leads to both the ceramics studio and the garage?" Sammy asked, peering into the backyard.

"I guess," I said.

"That's very helpful," she said. "Very, very helpful."

Our plan was for me to knock on the studio door and ask for my mother, who wouldn't be there because it was Monday and she teaches at Art4Kids on Mondays. Then, if Rob invited us in, we'd look around and say how cool everything was, thank him, and leave. This was Plan A.

"If Rob asks us any questions, we don't answer directly," Sammy instructed. "A good detective *gets* information, but *gives* zero."

The thing about the number zero is that it can be incredibly sneaky. Zero seems all round and sweet and "oh, nothing," but really, it can be very powerful.

First of all, zero is an identity thief, which means that any number you multiply by it becomes zero itself. *Any* number, no matter how huge: zero, in one instant.

Second, if zero is the exponent to any number, then that number is immediately reduced to one: $100°=1; 1,000,000°=1$.

And third, don't try putting zero in the denominator of a fraction, because then the fraction can't even exist.

So if it turned out we were doing Plan A, I was thinking it would be a good idea to be like a zero. I wanted to be all round and sweet and "Oh, nothing, just checking to see if my mom's here," but really I was going to be using my power to check out Rob.

Plan B—if Rob wasn't there—included looking in the garage itself. We'd try to see, for example, how airtight it was, or if there were any signs that there had been a fight in it, or, well, I didn't really know what else we were looking for.

"A cat!" Sammy said, grabbing my elbow and tugging me a little bit up the driveway. "A *living* cat," she whispered. As we watched the large gray animal run in front of us, I stood still. I knew at that second that I didn't want to sneak into the backyard or the studio or the garage; I knew I didn't want to pretend my mother worked there on Mondays when she didn't.

"Wait," I said, but Sammy kept walking.

"We're not doing anything wrong, Tess," she said. "We're just here to look for evidence that's in plain view."

Actually, everything was in plain view, because when we got to the door of the studio, it was wide open and there was Rob. He was wearing jeans and a blue T-shirt, and his hands were filled with clay. He didn't look like a killer. He looked like some tired guy, making pottery by himself.

On a big table right in front of us were two framed mirrors my mother had made. I knew they had to be hers because she's been working on these ceramic frames that have different parts of faces—eyes, noses, lips, chins, maybe even an eyebrow—floating around on them. Then you look in the mirror and you see your own face parts, and everyone kind of smiles when they do that, which is a nice way to look in a mirror.

"Hi, Tess," Rob said. "How are you?"

"I'm okay," I answered, and then I felt totally

weird. I mean, if someone's wife just died, you're supposed to give your sympathy and say, "I'm sorry to hear about your wife," and all, but if the man killed her himself, well, then what's the point of that? I'm sure nobody said, "Sorry to hear about your wife" to Henry the Eighth.

"This is my friend, Sammy," I said. "We were just taking the bus around here anyway, so we thought we'd come see my mom, but I guess she's not here." Then I pointed to a couple small figures on a shelf that looked like the elves on the front stairs. "Those are really cute," I said, before I finally shut up. I was trying to be all sweet and zerolike, but I sounded like an idiot.

"I've not seen your mom since last week," Rob said. "I haven't been to work since my wife died."

"Oh. I'm sorry. Okay, well, bye then," I said as the phone in Rob's pocket rang.

"This gets tricky," he said, wiping his wet, sticky hands on his jeans, reaching into his pocket, and flipping open his phone.

Sammy and I sort of waved good-bye before we turned and walked out. The door to the garage was only about two feet away, and it was open, too. The car Nina died in wasn't in there—well, I don't know what car she died in—but there was no car in the garage. There was nothing at all, except an old, broken kiln and a big pile of rags.

"That's a lot of rags," Sammy said. "That's enough rags to plug up all the cracks in a garage and make it airtight," she said.

"Come on," I said, grabbing her hand.

And then we both heard Rob's laughter. "Oh, how wonderful!" he said into his phone, and laughed more—deep, happy-sounding laughter, which made Sammy squeeze my hand hard.

As soon as we were all the way down the driveway, Sammy said exactly what I was thinking. "He sure doesn't sound like a man who's sad his wife just died."

Even though I agreed with her, that didn't seem fair. "You're allowed to laugh after someone you love dies," I said.

"What about the *cat*?" she asked. "It's obviously *not* dead."

"We don't even know if it's his," I said. "Cats go through other peoples' yards all the time."

"It's his," Sammy said.

It's true that sometimes a zero has a lot of power to change things, but at other times, a zero is just nothing. Even though I knew Sammy thought we'd gathered evidence against Rob, I didn't think so. I felt like we'd accomplished the second kind of zero—the nothing kind.

"Nothing" is also what I said at dinner when my father asked what was new, and what I said when my mother asked what I'd done after school.

Chapter 9
Percentages

Lynn and I are the only two people from Westlake who take the number 51 bus to school, which is why people think we're friends.

But the reason I can't stand her is because whenever somebody tells her something special happened to them, she says, "Oh, yeah, the same thing happened to me."

One stupid example is the other day at lunch when Sammy was telling us that her mother had once been a professional dancer, and then Lynn said that *her* mother used to dance for the San Francisco Ballet. ("How come we never heard about that before?" Miranda sort of mumbled while we all looked down at our food.) And, even stupider, when Taisha started seeing this guy who goes to Oakland High, Lynn said she had a boyfriend there, too, which everyone knew was a complete lie.

The girl is crazy.

My code for Lynn is the letter "y" because, in a linear equation, every time you substitute a different number for x, the y changes itself. Say the equation is y=2x+4. Then when x=1, y is 6, but when x=3, y is 10; y is always changing, depending on what the rest of the equation does, which is exactly like Lynn.

So when she was sitting next to me on the bus and said, "My mom knows about a murder," it really freaked me out. Because I knew exactly what it meant: It did *not* mean that Lynn's mother knew about a murder; it meant that Sammy hadn't kept her big mouth shut.

In the back of my notebook, I've figured out the

percentages of a lot of things. For example, there are sixteen girls in algebra (48% of the class), and three of them (19%) have boyfriends (counting Miranda, not counting Lynn). There are eighteen boys (52% of the class), and not one of them (0%) says he has a girlfriend.

But there's no way I could keep an exact score to figure out how much Lynn lies, so I'm just guessing when I say that I think it's about 60% of the time. For every ten things she says, six are probably lies.

Almost everyone else on the morning bus gets off before we do, so it was nearly empty when I asked Lynn who had been murdered.

"What?" she said, staring out the window like she'd never seen the car dealerships we pass every single day.

"Who's dead?" I snapped.

"Some guy my mother works with," Lynn said. "His wife."

"Yeah, right," I said.

You'd think someone who lies 60% of the time

would be better at it. But I knew that this discussion had nothing to do with Lynn's mother, and I knew, too, because Lynn and Sammy aren't friends even a little bit, that the reason Lynn didn't know who was dead was that Sammy hadn't told *her* the story. Sammy had told someone else, who probably told someone else, who had told Lynn.

We both stood up then, and I felt my legs sort of trembling as I walked off the bus thinking about what I could do to get back at Sammy.

First, though, I had to be positive that she had betrayed me. Because there was also the chance— maybe like 3%—that Miranda was the one who had broken her promise.

Chapter 10

The Quadratic Equation

I turned away from Lynn the second we got off the bus, and she didn't even try to talk to me anymore. The bell rang just as I got to the school parking lot, so I walked on my shaky legs right past Damien, who was sort of smiling at me, and right past Miranda, who said, "Nice shirt," which was not really a compliment since the light gray shirt with the white sleeves I was wearing used to be hers.

The first period of the day is algebra, and the first few minutes of algebra is called Do Now, which means that you sit at your seat, take out your spiral notebook, and work the problem on the screen until Ms. Saltzman turns off the quiet music that she thinks helps us calm down.

Today's Do Now said, "Solve: $y=x^2-2x-3$."

The only reason I hate quadratic equations is that there are a lot of ways to solve them, and you don't know which one you're supposed to use if nobody tells you. Sometimes the directions will say, "Solve by factoring" or "Solve by completing the square," so fine. But if it just says, "Solve," then you can sit there a long time wondering, Okay, great, but what exactly am I supposed to do?

That's how I was feeling. I was thinking about what my so-called friends had done, and I was wondering: What exactly am I supposed to do?

"Okay," Ms. Saltzman said when she turned off the music, "where do you want to start with this one?"

I could start with Miranda, I thought, and I wrote (1) $|m|$, in my spiral notebook. Miranda has been my supposed best friend all through middle school, and if someone is your supposed best friend, you should be able to ask her straight out: Did you break your promise? Did you talk about my private business with other people?

Taisha said she'd substitute numbers for x and sketch the graph, and it must not have been the best way to begin, because Ms. Saltzman nodded and said, "Yes, we could do that. Anyone have another approach?"

Another approach would be (2) s^5. I could write Sammy a note that said, "How would you like it if I told people *your* secrets—about how you wish you had a dancer's body like your mom? How would you like that, huh?"

There's no reason to start with (3) y, because Lynn will just lie.

When Marcus raised his hand and asked, "Why are we supposed to care about this?" which is the same question he always asks, people laughed.

But Ms. Saltzman took it seriously, of course.

"When we graph a quadratic equation, we get a parabola," she said moving her arm so that her pointed finger made the shape of a huge smile in the air. "Or this way," she said, air-drawing a frown, "which is the path all objects make when they are thrown into the air. The football you throw, the tennis ball you hit, the rock you skip over a lake—even the water that spurts from a fountain—as long as there is gravity, they will travel in the shape of a parabola." You could see, as Ms. Saltzman looked around the room, that she was completely thrilled about the concept of parabolas.

I wasn't. Not today.

"How can we figure out how far and how fast objects will travel?" Ms. Saltzman asked, and even though nobody answered her question, she said, "Yes! We use a quadratic equation!"

Then she looked at Marcus, and said, "We care, Marcus, because this is the beginning of the study of *physics*." She was sort of whispering when she said the word. "Quadratic equations are *very* important," Ms. Saltzman said, "because they are the way we can trace the path of a moving object."

Okay, great. But what I wanted to know was this: How can you trace the path of gossip? How do you know who started it, how far it went, and who else in the school knows your secret? If you want to tell me something *very* important, I thought, you could tell me the formula for *that*.

Ms. Saltzman put six quadratic equations on the screen after she finished her joy-of-parabolas lecture and said, "Raise your hand when you're done and I'll come stamp your work. Today I've got a Fibonacci spiral that's quite remarkable."

When Ms. Saltzman stamps your paper, it means you get credit. But when she started walking around the room with her ink pad, the only thing that was written in my spiral notebook was

1) $|m|$

2) s^5

3) y

I didn't even notice Ms. Saltzman until she was standing right next to my desk.

"What's your deal today, Tess?" she said.

"My *deal*?" I asked.

"Yeah. Where are you?" Ms. Saltzman asked. "Because you are definitely not in this classroom." Then she stamped a Fibonacci spiral on the papers of the three other people who sit in my cluster and walked away.

I'm pretty sure that today was the first time in my life I didn't get credit for my work in math class.

I'm absolutely sure it was the first time I didn't care.

Chapter 11
Parallel Lines

In fourth period I gave Sammy a note that said, "How does Lynn know about my mother? Huh?"

Sammy sits two seats behind me so I could watch her unfold the note and read it. She shook her head and looked all blank, like: *How would I know?* Then she wrote back, "The banner you made for the dance looks soooo great. Remember—today after school we have to finish painting everything."

I knew then, without a doubt, that it was Sammy who had betrayed me. When someone changes the subject to compliment you, you pretty much know for sure that they're trying to get away with a lie.

"Coincidences *do* happen," Miranda said when I told her at lunchtime. We were outside on the playground, standing behind the Dumpster. "I mean, maybe Lynn's mother really *does* know about a murder. There have been like a hundred of them in Oakland so far this year."

"Don't you think that would be a little *too* much of a coincidence, even for you, if a guy Lynn's mother works with killed *his* wife the exact same time that a guy my mother works with killed *his* wife?"

"What do you mean, 'even for me'?" Miranda asked.

There were two stones on the ground, and when I moved my feet so the stones were under my shoes, it felt like I was wearing high heels. "I mean that you're always making everything okay, even when it's not okay," I said, looking at my feet.

"I do not do that," Miranda snapped. "I just

don't think Sammy would break her promise, that's all."

James came over to us then and stood about two inches away from Miranda. I got off my high-heeled stones and, just as the bell rang, I kicked one of them against the metal wall of the Dumpster, which made James laugh, even though it wasn't funny at all.

Damien has science fifth period and I have it sixth, and when I got there, he was standing at the door of the classroom. "Hey," he said when I got near, and for a second I wished I could tell him that even though Miranda and Sammy and I had sealed our secret, they had broken the trust. I just said, "Hey," back to him, and then Mr. Lee waved me into the room.

History is the last class of the day. I didn't pay any attention to whatever Mr. Wright was talking about, I didn't listen to Sammy be brilliant, and I didn't even look up when Eddie, who sits right next to me, drummed on his desk with his pencils until Mr. Wright told him this was not jazz band practice. I just sat there staring at the "Citizen's Responsibilities" poster that's been hanging on the wall all year.

Sometimes I'm a little compulsive. By that I mean that there are things I feel I *have* to do even if they don't make sense. And what I felt as Mr. Wright talked about a more perfect nation, blah, blah, blah, was that I *had* to stay after class to ask him if it was one of my Citizen's Responsibilities to report a possible murder.

"Before I forget," Mr. Wright said about two seconds before the bell rang, "I've got to cancel boys' soccer practice today. Sorry, guys," he said, "but I have to take my car to that shop on the corner of Harrison and Webster before five o'clock, so no practice today. Please help me pass the word around to the rest of the team."

While I waited for everyone else to leave the room, I thought about Mr. Wright trying to get his car in on time. I knew he'd never find the corner of Harrison and Webster because those two streets are parallel, and sorry, but parallel lines just don't meet—not at a tire dealer or anyplace else in this world. And I wondered why, if I wanted to talk to someone I could trust, I would choose Mr. Wright, who doesn't even know the difference between parallel and perpendicular.

After everyone else was gone, I walked over to Mr. Wright's desk and watched him leaf through a huge stack of papers.

"Could I ask you a question about Citizen's Responsibilities?" I said.

"Sure," he answered, without looking up.

"I was just wondering, if you know about a crime, is it one of your Citizen's Responsibilities to tell the police?"

Mr. Wright had gone through each paper, but he must not have found what he was looking for because he began at the top of the pile again. "What do you know?" he asked.

And then, for about a minute, it seemed like I had forgotten about Rob and the possible murder, and was going to tell Mr. Wright about Richard and the stolen test.

While Mr. Wright looked at the papers, I stood in

front of him swallowing hard because my throat had started aching at that second, which sometimes means I'm getting really sick.

"It's not me," I said, after my next swallow, "it's my mother. Her friend might have murdered his wife."

That stopped Mr. Wright. He looked up from the papers and said, "Want to tell me what's going on?"

It turns out that Mr. Wright knew who Rob was because he'd seen his work in art galleries, and he knew about Nina's death because he'd read her obituary in the newspaper. But what Mr. Wright didn't know, of course, were the creepy things Rob had said when he'd told my mother about Nina's supposed suicide. Mr. Wright didn't know that Nina had had a lot of money.

"I assume your mother doesn't feel comfortable calling the police," Mr. Wright said.

"Yes," I said, worried that he was going to side with her.

"But you think she should report him?" Mr. Wright asked.

"I do," I said. "I'm not saying that he did it. I'm

just saying that there should be an investigation."

Mr. Wright looked back down at the pile of papers. "Could you see if Thomas's homework is in here?" he asked. "He swears he handed in the freedom of speech project, but I don't see it anywhere."

Then, while I looked at the name at the top of every paper, Mr. Wright stood up and walked back and forth by the windows.

"I have a friend," Mr. Wright finally said, "who might be helpful. Why don't I ask her a few questions about this situation."

"Is she a cop?" I asked.

"No," Mr. Wright said. "But she works with different police departments. I won't use your mother's name or yours—I'll just gather a little data, if you'd like me to do that."

"I'd really like it," I said. "Also, could you ask her to find out if there was a cat that died in the car, too?" I asked. Then I handed Mr. Wright a project with no name on it. "Maybe this one is Thomas's."

"I'll bet it is." Mr. Wright nodded. "Great."

I shoved my history book in my backpack and zipped it up, but before I left the room, I felt I had to say one more thing. "Harrison and Webster are parallel," I told Mr. Wright. "You can't bring your car to a shop on that corner, because there can't be a corner."

For some reason Mr. Wright found his mistake very funny. "Thank you, Tess," he said when he stopped laughing.

Mr. Wright is one of the only people I know who doesn't seem to feel bad when he's wrong. He doesn't seem to mind at all that he's stupid about math.

In the hallway outside the cafeteria, Sammy had unrolled my banner and about six people were painting my letters blue and red. Miranda was kneeling right next to Sammy and they had their heads close together so, if they wanted to, they could whisper while they painted.

You don't have to walk through the hallway outside the cafeteria to leave the building. You can turn around and walk in the opposite direction to the back door, which is what I did. I left everyone paint-ing the letters I had designed, and I walked out of the building. I walked past some of the boys from the soccer team sitting on the field not practicing, and I walked past Lynn standing at the bus stop waiting for the number 51 bus. I walked past my father's favorite burrito place on Twenty-third and past the video store on Thirty-fifth. I kept walking all the way to Forty-ninth Street until, about an hour later, I walked into my house.

Chapter 12

A Complete Circle

There's one thing you can throw that doesn't travel in the path of a parabola, and that's a boomerang. If you throw it correctly, it flies around a complete circle which, Ms. Saltzman says, is one more reason why physics is so fascinating. "That formula is $F=mv^2/r$, where F is force, m is mass, v is velocity, and r is the radius of the circle it travels. Amazing, isn't it, the mathematics of movement?"

I wish I'd thought about the path of a boomerang

before I told anybody anything. I wish I'd thought of the information coming right back home.

I knew something was wrong the minute I walked into the house and I heard the tone of my mother's voice. "Come to the kitchen, Tess," she called. "Now."

I knew something was *very* wrong when my mother turned off the water, turned away from the sink, and looked at me with angry, squinted eyes. "How does Laura Silver know about Nina's death?" she asked.

"Maybe there was an obituary in the newspaper," I said, as if I were just guessing, as if Mr. Wright hadn't told me that exact thing one hour ago.

My mother wiped her hands on her jeans and shook her head. "That's not what I meant. I meant, how does

Laura know I suspect Rob could have been involved?"

Laura Silver is Lynn the liar's mother. The reason Lynn and I are both on the number 51 bus is that we live on the same block.

"I have no idea," I answered.

"Tess, this is nobody's business," my mother said, and her voice was all quivery, like it gets when she's upset. When my mother is really furious, it sounds like someone is holding her by the shoulders and shaking her while she's trying to speak. *"Nobody's,"* she quivered. "I asked you not to repeat what I told you because I didn't want to start rumors, and now I have that fool Laura Silver coming up to me in the front yard and saying, 'Well, I hear there's been some drama in your life.' *Drama,*" my mother repeated, looking disgusted.

My mother is not the kind of person to scream, but if she were, she would have been screaming at me. If she were, she probably would have screamed at Laura Silver, too. My mother doesn't like Laura any more than I like Lynn.

"Why, oh, why," my mother asked in her non-screaming, furious quiver, "did you tell that girl my feelings?"

"I didn't."

"Tess," my mother said.

"I told Sammy and Miranda."

"And who else?"

"No one else," I said, even though one hour ago, I had told Mr. Wright. But I could never say that. I couldn't tell my mother that that was how I knew Nina's obituary had been in the newspaper, and I couldn't tell her that Mr. Wright was going to talk to a friend who worked with the police department. "Really, Mom—nobody else," I said, exactly like that liar Lynn.

My mother turned away from me and put the water back on then, which meant she didn't want to speak to me or look at me anymore, and that felt about ten thousand times worse than being screamed at. It felt like the boomerang had come back and hit me right in the stomach.

Chapter 13

The Number Line

"Why don't we get all the junk out of the garage," my father asked my mother at dinner, "and you can set up your own work space out there?"

My father said it casually, like it didn't mean anything important, but of course it did. It meant that my mother wasn't going to work at Rob's studio anymore, which was pretty much admitting that she thought he killed Nina, because if a man's wife dies any other way, you don't stop working with him.

My mother poured some dressing on the salad,

and while she mixed it up with two big wooden forks, I watched the lettuce bounce around and got very scared. I started to think that maybe she would talk to Rob and find out that Sammy and I went to his place and then she'd ask me in her quivery, angry voice, *"Why did you do that, Tess?"*

After my mother served herself some salad, she shook her head. "Thanks," she said to my father, "but I don't think there's enough light in the garage."

"I'm not so sure about that," Dad said. "Remember that huge window is covered by cardboard boxes filled with god-knows-what. Think about it," he encouraged. "We could clean it out this weekend—Tess'll help too," he offered without asking me. Then he squirted some mustard all over his hamburger, plopped the bun on top, and passed the bright yellow container to me.

"I hate mustard," I told him.

"Really?" he asked, all shocked, like he hadn't been eating dinner with me for thirteen years.

"Really," I answered. "Also," I said, reaching for the

ketchup bottle, "I don't exactly want to spend my weekend cleaning out the garage."

"Let me ask you a question," Dad said, slicing his hamburger in half before he picked it up. "Is there some sort of rule book I don't know about that says it's a *requirement* for you to have a negative attitude now that you're a teenager?"

I knew this was supposed to be a joke, but it wasn't the least bit funny, so I pounded out some ketchup and said, "There's nothing wrong with being negative."

"Pardon me?" my father asked.

This was another one of those times when I should have shut up, but instead I said, "Negative numbers just go a different direction on the number line. They go to the left of zero and positive numbers go to the right of zero."

My father picked up his wineglass, took a sip, and looked at me.

"Say you want to take BART from the stop closest to school," I explained, giving the exact same example Ms. Saltzman had used when she talked about the number line. "The Nineteenth Street station would be your starting point, so that would be labeled zero because you don't have to travel at all to get there. Three stops west would be negative three, and three stops east would be positive three, but that doesn't mean that Ashby is any better than Fruitvale."

"Now you're losing me," Dad said.

I was sort of losing myself, too, but still I went on talking because maybe my mother had already spoken to Rob and she was just waiting for the right time to ask, "Why did you do that, Tess?" Talking about the number line was much, much better than getting hit in the stomach with a boomerang again.

"So your saying I have a 'negative attitude,'" I told my father, "is like saying that I have a 'west' attitude, which, of course, means nothing."

"Are you following this?" Dad asked Mom.

My mother reached for her own wineglass then and shook her head like, no, she wasn't following it, and furthermore she didn't care one bit about the whole conversation.

Even my father stopped talking then, and as soon as I finished my hamburger, I cleared my plate and left the table.

When Miranda called and asked why I hadn't shown up to paint my poster, I told her I couldn't talk because my father was making me clean out the garage, and when Sammy sent me an IM that said, "Hey, girl, you there?" I typed back "No" and signed off.

Then I went up to my room and tried really hard not to cry. Because even if Ms. Saltzman is right about numbers, it's very different when you're talking about feelings—the positive ones *are* better than the negative ones. I mean, of course it's better to be happy than to be depressed. It feels awful when you and your mother are so angry you're hardly speaking to each other, or when you learn that your friends aren't really your friends. And it might seem stupid, but you can feel very sad when some lady you hardly even know is dead in her own garage.

I sat down on the floor of my room then, and on the inside of my left ankle, right below the bone, I drew a thick black minus sign in the center of a small dark circle. It was a big negative, and it was the symbol that meant me.

Chapter 14
Prime Numbers

It's pretty easy to get through a day at my school without really talking to anyone if you don't want to. On the bus Wednesday morning, I sat in a seat with an old man so that big-mouth liar Lynn couldn't sit next to me, and at lunch I went to Ms. Saltzman's classroom so Sammy and Miranda couldn't say, "What's your problem, Tess?"

Ms. Saltzman has "chew and chat" time every Wednesday where you can bring your lunch and get tutoring, and even though I had a hundred on last week's test, she acted like it was normal for me to be there with the kids who had flunked. After I finished eating, Ms. Saltzman asked me if I wanted to check the thirty classroom calculators to see which needed new batteries, because everyone was complaining about dead calculators.

The only time the whole day I didn't feel completely negative was for a couple seconds when I saw Damien standing by the door of the science room again. "Rockets today," he said before he left for his next class, which did make me smile a little.

Miranda is in sixth period science, though, and she kept looking in my direction, like she was wondering what was wrong.

Also, in history class, Mr. Wright was very annoying. He usually wears clothes you'd never notice, but today he was wearing this fancy Hawaiian shirt with red and yellow flowers all over it, and he was standing at the doorway to the classroom welcoming everyone as if we'd come to his house for a birthday party or something.

"Good afternoon, Tess, Ryan, Yamel. New haircut, Henry? Looking good—looking very good. Hello there, Sammy." Seriously, like we were guests at his home, and he was the greatest host ever.

Maybe it *is* his birthday, I thought, as I sat down.

When everyone had been properly greeted, Mr. Wright sort of danced into the room, and wrote the numbers 192, 77, 4, and 100 on the board.

Then he stood smiling in front of the classroom until we were all quiet and said, "Okay, look at these numbers, class, because they tell quite a remarkable story. These are *prime numbers*."

Of all the stupid math things that Mr. Wright has ever said, this one might be the stupidest. I bet every other person in this room, except for the teacher, knew that a prime number was a number, like 5 or 17, that can't be divided by any other number except 1 and itself. So none of those numbers on the board could possibly be prime. (I mean, *100*? You can divide 100 by 2, 4, 5, 10, 20, 25, 50. It's about as far away from being a prime number as you can get.)

Mr. Wright picked up the silver pointer that sits in the chalkboard tray and tapped it against the number 192. "This is how many eighth graders there are at Westlake." Then he tapped the next number. "There were seventy-seven questions on the U.S. Constitution exam." Mr. Wright smiled before he tapped the number 4 and said, "This is the number of students *in this very class* who got," and here Mr. Wright paused to move his pointer around in a circle as if he were a magician about to bring a live rabbit out of a hat, "you guessed it—100 percent."

So that's what the Hawaiian shirt and the happiness were about: Mr. Wright was ecstatic about the results of the U.S. Constitution test. "Never in my twelve years of teaching," he told us, writing the number 12 (also not prime) beneath the others, "has anyone ever scored perfectly on this exam, and I am honored to congratulate the four of you!"

Everyone else in the class got all excited to find out who the perfect people were. Marcus started giggling for no reason, Richard took the tip of his blue pen and darkened the phony tattoo on his left wrist, and Sammy looked like she could hardly breathe.

"Luis," Mr. Wright said, nodding at him, "Eddie, Richard, and Sammy, will you come to the front of the room, please?"

While everyone but me was clapping for the geniuses, I stared at Richard's phony tattoo and then, just on a hunch, I looked at Luis's and Eddie's wrists. When I saw the exact same tattoos, my heart started to race, and even before I checked it out, I knew that Sammy's left wrist would be clean.

Mr. Wright returned the tests to the rest of us who were < perfect, and after I shoved mine into my backpack (an 87, which isn't prime because you can divide it by 3), I took out my math notebook, flipped to the back, and wrote:

s^5=100%,

but the 3 ">"≠100%

which meant: Sammy (who does know history even if she doesn't know how to be a friend) really did get a perfect score because she knew all the

answers, but the three boys who think they're supposed to be > other people, don't know 100 percent
of anything.

Eddie's desk is about two feet away from mine, so
the whole time Mr. Wright was going around the
room passing back the tests and speaking to individ-
ual people, I tried to study Eddie's wrist without
being too obvious. The tattoo looked like a bracelet.
It was made up of two dark blue curvy lines that
twisted across each other and formed these small
loops. Inside each of the loops (well, I couldn't see
inside *each* of them, but the ones I could see), there
were dots. Some loops had one dot and some had
more.

I know a code when I see one, and I would bet
anything that I was seeing one.

And I would also bet that this is pretty much
exactly what happened: Richard showed the stolen
test to Luis and Eddie, and the three of them looked
up all the right answers in the history book and
made cheat sheets. Then someone, maybe Eddie,

made the code, and Luis did some fancy artwork, and now they were all *wearing those cheat sheets on their wrists*. I would bet any amount of money in the world that the answers to the U.S. Constitution exam were woven into the designs of the phony bracelet tattoos.

Mr. Wright clapped his hands to get our attention, or maybe he wanted us all to applaud a second time. "Historical Events of the Twentieth Century," he announced, picking up his red marker. "What more do we need to add to our time line?"

"Marcus Foster Coleman's birthday," Marcus called out, which some people, of course, thought was hysterical.

"Well, how about that?" Mr. Wright said, surprised. "I didn't realize that was your full name, Marcus. I suspect your parents named you after someone in history whom they greatly admired. Am I right about that?"

Marcus nodded.

"Do you want to tell the class who another Marcus Foster was?"

"He was a guy who ran the Oakland schools and was murdered."

"Yes," Mr. Wright agreed, and by the year 1968 on the time line he wrote: *Dr. Marcus Foster appointed Oakland's first African-American superintendent of schools.* "Dr. Foster was a talented educator and a remarkable man," Mr. Wright said, "and how special for his name to inspire Marcus and the rest of us today!"

Marcus took a phony little bow at his desk, but you could see that he liked what Mr. Wright was saying. You could see that everyone else in class was having a very good time today.

"Other dates from recent history?" Mr. Wright asked, and Taisha said, "December sixteenth is the winter dance," which was also supposed to be funny.

"No matter how important it may be to you," Mr. Wright said, smiling, "I doubt that we'll be able to label it a historical event. Also," he said, "let's remember that history is the study of what has already happened, not what we're planning."

"Four perfect scores already happened," Eddie said, and Mr. Wright laughed aloud.

"*That*," he said, "might just qualify as a historic event!"

Sammy smiled, Richard shook both his fists in the air, and I dug the tip of my pencil into a hole in the top of my desk until the point snapped off.

If you want to talk about prime anything, I thought as I looked up at Mr. Wright, you could talk about *prime suspects*. And if you want to write a real prime number on the board, you could write the number 3, which is the exact number of people in this very class who cheated their way into "a historical event."

Chapter 15

One More DNE

On Thursday Mr. Wright was completely different. He was back to wearing his regular clothes—a light gray shirt and dark gray pants—and he didn't greet us at the door. Instead, he was sitting at his desk, and after we came in and sat down, he walked to the front of the class and looked down at his shoes.

"Here's another number we need to talk about," he said, and wrote 42 on the board.

There was something in the way Mr. Wright spoke, quiet and sad-sounding, that made everyone in the class shut up and listen. It looked like we were playing that game where when you call out "freeze," everyone has to stop moving at that exact second.

Even Mr. Wright stood still, staring at the back of the room like he was trying to figure out exactly what he wanted to say. Which was weird, because last night my father had seemed just like that all through dinner—like he wanted to say something to me, but didn't know how to say it. My father thinks that you should always "talk through your problems," so it was unusual for him to let me sit there without speaking during the whole meal.

"Okay," Mr. Wright finally said, "I will tell you something you don't know, and then I will ask you to tell me something I don't know."

Everyone was still pretty frozen. Without moving anything except my eyeballs, I could see the back of Richard's head, and I could see Eddie's wrist, so I knew he'd washed off his tattoo bracelet.

"The thing you don't know," Mr. Wright said, "is that every test we get from the state is numbered."

Silence, still.

"When we get the tests back, we do two things. First of all, we make sure every eighth grader took the test, and second, we make sure every test is accounted for. Today I learned that number forty-two is missing."

The classroom still stayed silent, and I think people were trying to figure out why test number forty-two was so important.

"Why does it matter if it's missing?" Marcus finally asked.

I knew exactly why it mattered, though, and so did Richard.

Mr. Wright answered Marcus with the same question. "Why *does* it matter?" he asked the class.

"Because it means someone stole a test," Sammy answered. "Someone cheated."

Mr. Wright looked from Sammy to Marcus, then at every other person in the room before he said, "Yes. This is not only cheating. This is also stealing. At Westlake School we take this very, very seriously."

Lynn sort of shocked me then, because she said what a lot of people were probably thinking, but for the first time in her life she didn't wait for someone else to say it and then just agree. "Maybe it was the people who got a hundred," she said.

"That's not fair!" Sammy said. "That's sooooo not fair!"

And for the first time in *his* life, Mr. Wright seemed to think Sammy might have given the wrong answer.

"It's a logical assumption," he said to Lynn, "but we don't want accusations without just cause." Then he looked around the room some more and said, "Sometimes people who steal tests make sure they don't get a hundred."

You could just see, if you were looking at the back of Richard's head, that that really got to him. He was lower in his seat and his arms were folded all tight on his chest, and even from behind, you could see that he hated himself that he hadn't thought to cheat less.

"I will be in this classroom until five o'clock

today," Mr. Wright said, "and Ms. Balford will also be in her office. Anyone who would like to speak to either of us about the situation will have until that time."

Every single person in the room was wondering what would happen after five o'clock, but nobody, not even Marcus, asked the question.

"I would like all supplemental reading books returned by that time as well, so check your lockers and backpacks after school today."

Very clever, I thought, as Mr. Wright turned on the overhead projector and slipped a list of words onto the screen, because now people wouldn't know if you were coming into his room after school to tattle or to return a book. Very clever, Mr. Wright.

"Due process," he said pointing to the first phrase on the list. "That's a good place for you to start today. You may use your textbooks to look up the definition for each of the terms on this list."

I thought Mr. Wright was finished talking when he sat down at his own desk, but then he said one more thing. "It will, of course, be a great deal better for all concerned if the person or people responsible for this crime come forward themselves."

While I was staring at my history book, Lynn did it again.

"What happens if nobody comes forward by five o'clock?" she asked.

"If nobody comes forward," Mr. Wright said, "Ms. Balford and I have decided that the only fair solution is to have everyone in the eighth grade retake the test. That will happen the day after tomorrow."

Nobody was silent then. Nearly every single person, except for Richard, Eddie, and Luis, said, "What!" or "No fair!" or "I'm not taking that thing again!" until Mr. Wright held up his hand.

"You have work to do" was all he said, and everyone shut up.

After class, when I went to my locker to get my supplemental reading book, I saw a piece of folded green paper tucked into the side of the metal door. Miranda is very good at origami—she can fold anything to look like a swan or a turtle or even a rose, and this one was the turtle, which is my favorite. I unfolded the little turtle to see if Miranda had written me a note, but there were no words on either side of the paper.

Mr. Wright was sitting at his desk when I walked into the empty room. It was 3:05, so there was only one hour and fifty-five minutes left. "Ah, Tess," he said, "I heard from my friend about your problem."

Which problem, I wondered as I handed Mr. Wright the book.

"Just put it on that pile," he said, looking through the top drawer of his desk until he found a piece of blue paper and unfolded it. "Here it is," he said, and read for a moment before he told me, "Jilliane says that in every case of suicide, they automatically make an investigation."

Oh, *that* problem.

"What they found in this case," Mr. Wright said,

reading from the paper, "was that 'the forty-four-year-old woman died of carbon monoxide poisoning. There was no evident trauma, or any other sign of struggle.'"

"So that means?" I asked.

"Well, I guess it means that the police have no proof that it was anything other than a suicide. It implies that Rob didn't kill his wife and then put her body in the car. She really did die of that poison going into her body. There's no physical evidence that anyone else was involved."

When Mr. Wright looked up from the note, he seemed very sad. Maybe that's because he'd been sad all day, but honestly, for a minute, I thought that if I weren't there he would have just put his head down on his desk and cried. "And yes," he said, "there was a cat in the car with her—an orange tabby. It died too." So the gray cat we saw meant nothing, I thought. It was probably just some random cat running through the neighborhood.

The door to Mr. Wright's classroom was closed,

but Eddie didn't bother to knock. He walked in and said, "You nearly finished talking to Tess?"

"Are other students waiting in the hall?" Mr. Wright asked.

"Just me," Eddie said, and he sounded nervous. Nervous like you'd be if you were going to tell Mr. Wright about the stolen test and cheat-sheet bracelets and wanted to do it quickly before anyone saw you or you lost your courage.

"Give me another few minutes," Mr. Wright said, then turned back to me as Eddie walked very, very slowly out of the room.

"Jilliane wanted me to tell you that she can just speak to the *scientific* part of the case. Especially with a suicide, there's an awful lot we'll never know. Even science doesn't tell the whole story sometimes," Mr. Wright said.

"In math, too," I said. "In math, sometimes the answer is DNE."

For the first time all day, Mr. Wright sort of smiled. "I told Jilliane that you were my math tutor.

But I thought I might get away without a lesson today." Then he held up one finger to Eddie, who had walked into the room again, and said, "I'll open the door when I'm ready," and turning back to me, said, "Okay, tell me what DNE means, please."

"Does Not Exist," I said. "Sometimes you can't find the answer to a problem because it's just DNE."

Mr. Wright nodded, stood up, and acted like he was finished talking to me. It seemed like he didn't think for one minute that I had come to tell him anything about the stolen test, so I stood up too and walked right past Eddie as he came in the door.

Chapter 16

Imaginary Numbers

Mathematicians really don't like it if too many answers are Do Not Exist, so sometimes they just invent a new concept so they can say they're solving the problem.

Seriously. Like, for example, there's no square root for a negative number, because any number multiplied by itself is positive. (The square root of 9 can either be 3, because 3x3=9, or −3, because (-3)(-3)=9, but there's no number you can multiply by itself to get −9.) So someone made up what's called an imaginary number, because you can only *imagine* what the square root of a negative number would be. Then they had to invent a way to write it, so they came up with *i*, which means imaginary. So the square root of −9 would be 3*i*.

I know it sounds like cheating, but actually I think it's a good idea, because there are plenty of things in this world that you can only imagine.

Suicide's one of them. Nobody who's alive can know what suicide is like.

The whole time I walked home from school—for the twenty-seven blocks of Broadway, anyway—I tried to imagine what happened that night. I imagined that Nina and Rob had a huge fight and she said something like, "I never should have come back to you," and he said, "I wish you hadn't."

I was walking past the new hospital when I imagined Nina telling Rob that she was going to kill herself. Rob thought about all her money that would be his if she were dead, and he said, "Fine, do it."

And then she went to the garage, and he didn't try to talk her out of it. He didn't say, "Nina, stop. I love you," or whatever, and so she went out there and set everything up. Maybe she put those exact rags Sammy and I saw around the base of the garage door so the poisonous gas wouldn't slip out and the fresh air wouldn't slip in. Then, before she got into the car, she went back into the house.

She looked at Rob lying on their bed reading a book and she said, "My feet are cold. I need my slippers."

"Why do you need your slippers if you're going to kill yourself?" he would have asked, all sarcastic, probably not believing she was really going to do it—because, like he said to Mom, why would you care if your feet were cold if you were about to die?

"Sarah knit them for me," Nina might have said, which made no sense to Rob, so he just shrugged.

Then Nina went back out to the garage and sat in the car breathing in that poison and the graph of her life ended.

That's one way it could have happened.

I was only about five blocks from my house when I remembered the cat, and wondered why Rob had told Mom that the cat was on the pillow at first, when it was really outside in the car, dead with Nina.

I stopped in front of the art supply store on the corner of Forty-ninth and Broadway and stared at the display of handmade papers while I thought about that one. What I thought was this: Maybe Mom was right not to tell the cops. Maybe the reason Rob had gone off on all those stupid tangents the morning of Nina's death really was because he was freaked that his wife had just died, so he didn't know what he was saying half the time.

Because if Nina's death happened anything like I was just thinking it happened, then Rob didn't commit any murder. And if Mom had told the police to do an investigation, then, even if Rob wasn't really guilty, a lot of people would still think he was. That's how gossip works—once it's out there, you pretty much always think it might be true. And maybe, like

Miranda said, the police would stay suspicious of Rob for the rest of his life.

When you look through a store window, you can either see what's on the other side or, if you focus your eyes a little differently, you can see your reflection instead. I was still looking in the art supply store window, but I wasn't looking at the handmade paper anymore—I was looking at myself, standing there with my hands in the pockets of my jeans skirt and my white T-shirt crumpled under the straps of my backpack. When I looked up at my face, I saw that Richard was standing behind me. "Tell me exactly what happened," he said right into my ear.

Broadway and Forty-ninth is a busy corner, so if Richard was trying to scare me, he picked the wrong place. There were two old ladies standing near me, and a jogger was bouncing up and down waiting for the light to change so he could jog across the street. For a second, maybe because I was too much in my imagination, I thought Richard was talking about

Rob which, when you think about it, is really weird.

"Eddie saw you talking to Mr. Wright," Richard said, "so don't pretend you don't know what I mean."

"What I talked about with Mr. Wright is none of your business," I said.

"You think you know something, but you don't," Richard said. "You don't know anything."

The light turned green then, and the old ladies and jogger crossed the street, but I stood there looking at Richard. "I know what I saw that day in the copy room," I told him.

"That's exactly what you don't know," Richard said, and then he looked around to make sure nobody heard, I guess. "And you don't know about your friend Sammy."

The light had become red again and now two mothers with babies in strollers stopped at the corner. "Sammy's not my friend," I said, even though that was none of Richard's business either.

"She likes Eddie," Richard said, "and she wants him to like her."

"So what?" I asked.

"So maybe she'd want to do a favor for him."

I hooked my thumbs around the straps of my backpack and looked directly at Richard's eyes. "Sammy didn't cheat, and you know it. She got a hundred because she knows everything about history."

The light turned green again and I stepped back a little so the strollers could go down the cutout part of the curb.

"It's cheating if you hold your test so people can see the answers," Richard said, staying close to me and smiling.

Then, all quiet and secretlike, he said, "Picture where our desks are. All the answers we didn't know came from Sammy—and it was *her* idea."

I did picture it: Eddie's desk is right behind Sammy's, and Luis and Richard are to his left, so, yes, it was possible.

"That's not what happened," I snapped. "You *stole* that test, Richard."

"That's what *you* say," he whispered.

Broadway has six lanes of traffic, so it's not the kind of street you can just run across. But I wanted to run now that I understood Richard's plan: He was going to try to pin the whole thing on Sammy so he only got punished for cheating—because if you got caught cheating, you'd probably just get an F for the test. But nobody knew what would happen to you if you got caught stealing. *That's* what Eddie was there to tell Mr. Wright—that Sammy had given them all the answers. And Richard was here to make sure I hadn't already told Mr. Wright that I'd seen him with the stolen test.

I wished I had. I wished I'd told Sammy, too, even though it was against her rules to tattle on a cheater.

"I know something else you might be interested in," Richard said, as I looked down Broadway and saw the number 51 bus coming. "Luis likes you."

Richard was so filled with lies, I didn't even say anything.

"He does," Richard said, all smiley and sweet and good-looking. "That's why he wants to ask you to go to the winter dance with him."

"I'm not going to the dance with anyone," I said. The light finally turned green one more time and the bus pulled up to its stop. And then, slowly, like it was no big deal, I started walking across the street, whispering, "Don't leave, don't leave, don't leave," to the bus.

I sort of ran the last few feet, though, because I was too scared to walk, and it was lucky I did, because the doors closed right after I got on that bus.

I didn't look out the window to see if Richard was watching, but I bet he was. And I bet it only took him a second to figure out that the bus I was on was heading right back to school.

Because even though it was probably after five o'clock, I had to tell Mr. Wright that the answer to the question of who stole test number 42 wasn't DNE and wasn't imaginary. The answer was real, and it was Richard.

Chapter 17
The Additive Property of Equality

It was the Additive Property of Equality that made me tell. It says that whatever you add to one side of an equation, you've got to add to the other; it says you've got to be fair.

If Richard was adding Eddie to his side, someone needed to be added to Sammy's side. So even though I'd hated her since last week, I felt I had to get on that bus.

The front door of Westlake was locked when I got there, but the one to the gym was still open, and Mr.

Henley was tossing trash into the Dumpster.

"I'm going to see Mr. Wright," I told him.

"Just left," he said, closing the big metal lid. "You'll need to catch him tomorrow."

"What about Ms. Balford?" I asked.

"You can check," Mr. Henley said, "but then you come right out this door if she's not there."

Ms. Balford was standing in front of her office door, her key in the lock, her cell phone to her ear. "Not in this school, we don't," she was saying. "In this school, the rules apply to everyone. Thank you for your call."

"Hello, Tess," she said, unlocking the door she'd just locked and acting like we had some sort of an appointment I didn't know about. She gestured for me to sit down and then sat in a chair next to mine, not the one behind her huge messy desk.

I guess she was ready to go home, so she didn't want to make any small talk. "Go ahead" was all she said.

"Sammy could have gotten that hundred," I said. "She didn't need to cheat."

"I suppose she could have." Ms. Balford nodded.

"It's not that she *could have*," I corrected us both. "It's that she *did*."

"So what is it that you're telling me, Tess?"

"That Sammy didn't cheat."

"Yes, I got that part. And how do you know this? Did Sammy tell you?"

"No, I'm not talking to Sammy," I said.

Ms. Balford let her cell phone ringer play the first bar of "When the Saints Come Marching In" before she reached to her belt and turned it off.

"Richard stole the test," I said. "And when you tell him you found out, he'll know I was the one who told you."

"Where did you get your information?" Ms. Balford asked.

I pointed to the wall that separates Ms. Balford's office from the closet where the Xerox machine is.

"From the copy room?" Ms. Balford asked, and after I nodded, she said, "What, exactly, did you see happen there?"

"I saw Richard make a copy of the U.S. Constitution test."

"Why do you think he was making a copy?" Ms. Balford asked.

"I think he meant to return the original to the pile on Mr. Wright's desk, but something must have happened because, well, obviously, Richard never got the stolen test back in that pile. Also, I saw something else," I said.

"Yes?"

"Richard and Luis and Eddie had these bracelet tattoos the day of the test, and I'm nearly positive that's where the answers were."

Ms. Balford straightened out her legs, folded her hands in front of her and looked up, like she needed to think for a little while.

"In code," I added.

"Did you know that others have already blamed Sammy?" Ms. Balford asked.

"Sort of," I said.

"And Richard will know it's you who told, because

131

he knows you saw him with the stolen test, right?"

"Yes."

"Do you have a sense of what he'll do about that?"

"Make people hate me," I said. "Tell everyone I'm a liar."

Ms. Balford nodded. "I'm curious, then," she said. "If you and Sammy aren't talking right now, do you mind my asking why you're telling, since the only reason to tell now is to save Sammy's behind?"

My backpack was on the floor by my feet, and I stared at it while I thought about what to say. It was too weird to try to explain that the Additive Property of Equality was the reason I was telling. It was too stupid to say that whatever you did to one side of an equation, you had to do to the other side, and that's how I wanted to be in my life—fair like that. Also, while I was sitting in Ms. Balford's office, I wasn't exactly positive that that *was* the real reason I wanted to help Sammy. Because I was also thinking that Sammy wouldn't have been able to break her promise to me if I hadn't broken my promise to my mother first. I was thinking that when someone's one of your best friends or your daughter, you're on her side even if she makes a really bad mistake.

But I didn't say any of that to Ms. Balford. I just said, "Mr. Wright was really excited about those perfect grades."

Ms. Balford's hand touched the back of mine and when I looked at her, she said, "Thank you for doing this, Tess. It's brave of you. We will be very clear with the boys who are responsible that there will be serious repercussions if they intimidate you in any way."

"Okay," I said, even though I knew it didn't matter what she said to them. Richard was the kind of person who would try to ruin my reputation just so he could be > me.

Ms. Balford sat back then, looked at her watch, and said, "Would you like to use my phone, so your family knows why you're so late?"

"Thanks." As soon as she turned on her phone and

handed it to me, it began playing music again, so I gave it right back. "Balford here," she answered. Then she stood up, turned her back to me, and said, "That's very interesting. Yes, I'd like them to come in at seven-thirty tomorrow morning to speak to me. I'm not certain what the punishment will be, but it will certainly be better if they come forward."

She faced me while she listened to the other person talk, and even though she smiled when she answered, there was nothing smiley in her voice when she said, "My concern is not with the basketball tournament, sir. Thank you for calling."

Mr. Henley put his head in the door of the office then, looked at me, and nodded. "Just checking to see if that child was in here," he said.

"She's here," Ms. Balford said. "Tess did something courageous, Mr. Henley, and now it looks like she's not going to have to be penalized for it. It looks like the boys involved have decided to do the right thing. Don't you love when that happens?"

"That's how it ought to be," Mr. Henley said as he

turned to leave. "But you sure can't count on it."

Ms. Balford must have forgotten that she was going to lend me her phone, because instead of giving it back to me, she asked me my home number. "Tess has been helping me," she told my mother, "and I'm afraid it's gotten very late, so I thought I'd give her a lift home. No, no problem at all. I'll drop her off soon. Good evening."

There are times you feel like reaching out and hugging a grown-up, but of course, you don't do it. You just pick up your backpack and walk out the office door while she stands there waiting to lock it again.

There are times, too, when you feel like making up with your best friend, but you're not sure how. So when I walked into the house and my mother told me Miranda had called, I sort of froze. "She said she wanted to ask you a question," Mom said, "but please wait until after dinner to call her because we're just about to eat."

Even before I sat at the table, my father asked

what I had helped Ms. Balford with, and I sort of summed up the whole cheating thing. My mother was mixing sauce into a bowl of spaghetti, but when I got to the part about Richard following me after school, she held the spoon in midair.

"Do you feel afraid of this boy?" she asked.

I shook my head and sat down. "He doesn't even know for sure that I told, because whoever called Ms. Balford when I was in the office told, too. I think it might have been his father," I said. "But still"—I shrugged—"Richard will probably say bad things about me."

Dad told a story about someone he knew who had gone to jail for cheating in business, but I didn't exactly hear him, because I was thinking about Miranda and wondering what she wanted to ask me.

I heard my mother, though, when she said, "I admire you, Tess."

"Thanks," I said, looking up from my spaghetti. Mom was smiling at me for the first time in a while, and I knew that she was on my side, and that it didn't have anything to do with the Additive Property of Equality.

Then I ate about two more bites and went to my room to call Miranda.

Usually when I don't know what to say I talk too much, and usually when Miranda is nervous she doesn't talk at all. But this time it seemed like we switched, because as soon as she heard my voice she said, "Luke got his license and he's driving Mom crazy, making all these excuses to borrow the car."

"That's awesome," I said.

"He's going to the store for milk now, and we don't even need it." Miranda sort of laughed when she said that, and I sort of laughed too.

Then, even though it had been three days since we'd spoken and I had wondered if we'd ever be close again, when Miranda said, "What's going on?" I closed the door to my room and whispered, "I told Mr. Wright about Rob and Nina."

"Are you serious?" Miranda whispered back.

"Yes," I said, crawling into the far corner of my bed, which is where I like to go to talk privately. I told Miranda all about Mr. Wright's friend, and the investigation and what the police report had said. "No evidence of trauma," I explained.

Miranda was quiet for a little while before she spoke. "I hate to say it, because Rob's a really good teacher and a nice person and all, but I still sort of believe your mom."

"Even though there was no 'sign of struggle'?"

"Even though," Miranda said. "I don't think your mom would feel suspicious for no reason, do you?"

"Not really," I said as I rubbed my thumb over the thick black minus sign I'd drawn on the inside of my ankle.

The question Miranda had called to ask me was if I wanted a ride to the winter dance because Luke had offered to drive, of course. "Can we pick you up Saturday night?"

"Sure," I said, leaning back against the cool

outside wall of my room. "Thanks."

I had to use nail polish remover to get the minus sign completely erased from my foot that night. Then, sitting on the floor of my room, I stared at the clean, soft spot right below my anklebone for a very long time.

Chapter 18
Extraneous Solutions

The days that you're suspended, you're not allowed to be in the building or do anything that's even related to the school. Sometimes you're lucky and there's nothing happening that you care about, but Richard, Luis, and Eddie were definitely not lucky.

That week they couldn't play in the basketball tournament, which was the biggest thing in their lives, and on Saturday night they had to miss the dance. If you're going to get yourself suspended, you should try to make sure you don't do it the week before winter break, because you lose out on too many important things.

Even though Mr. Wright completely believed that Sammy had nothing to do with the cheating, she sort of suspended herself. She didn't come to school on Friday and she didn't come to the dance Saturday night, and Miranda said there was no way she was sick.

The best parts of the winter dance didn't even take place at the actual dance. The first one was that my father gave me these beautiful silver hoop earrings to wear that night. We had spent the afternoon helping Mom empty out the garage, and I had just washed up after cleaning the filthy windows when Dad gave me a little satin bag with the earrings inside. He'd never bought me anything like that before and you could tell he was proud of himself that I liked them so much. "You look very lovely," he said, when I put the earrings on and started dancing around. "Very, very lovely."

The second thing was that when Luke picked me up, he was wearing a hat that made him look like a limo driver and he kept saying "At your service, ladies," to Miranda and me. He opened the car doors for us when we got to school and helped us out of the backseat like we were celebrities, and you could see that all the kids who were standing around the driveway thought it was very cool to have a driver who wasn't a parent.

When we got to the actual dance, Miranda and I just stood in the back of the room with some of the other girls for about the first half hour. Someone had hung my "Celebrate!" sign over the stage and there were silver streamers hanging from it. Right below it, a DJ in a T-shirt that looked like a tux jacket was playing music and trying to get people to have fun.

Miranda was wearing a shiny blue dress with a halter top that looked great on her. Her shoes were royal blue like the dress, and the heels were pretty high, but she walked like she was used to them. I walked okay in my shoes, but they weren't as high as Miranda's. They were black like my dress, and I felt sort of sophisticated in black everything. My mother had helped me put about a thousand curls in my ponytail, and even though Miranda said she loved it, I wasn't sure it looked that great.

"I wish Sammy was here," Miranda said, looking around the room. Then she turned toward me and said, "Some people still believe she cheated."

"Some people are idiots," I told her.

James came over to where we were standing and said, "Wow" when he looked at Miranda.

"I don't think Sammy cheated," Lynn's voice said from behind me.

When I spun around, the bottom of my dress twirled out. Lynn's red dress had thin straps that tied in small bows, and she had on red lipstick the same shade as her dress. "Was somebody talking to you?" I snapped.

The thing with Lynn is that she usually doesn't even know when you're being mean to her, but this time she did. She opened the tiny red purse she was carrying and pretended she needed something in there. "It's such a long walk home," she said into her purse, "but you do it instead of taking the bus now. How come?"

Lynn looked really good in red, and I sort of wished I wasn't being mean when we were both dressed so nice. But I had been angry too long to stop myself. "Maybe it's because I don't like the company on the bus," I said. "Maybe I didn't appreciate that you told your mother something that was none of her business or yours."

Lynn nodded and closed her purse. "That happened to me one time too," she said.

"It did not, Lynn."

"Yes, it did," she said, looking right at me. "I told Brandy that I thought my parents were breaking up and her mother told my mother she was sorry to hear about their divorce and there wasn't even a divorce."

Lynn opened her little red purse again, even though there was obviously nothing in it she needed, and said, "I hated Brandy for telling her mother, so I guess you hate me now."

I just shrugged, and then we both stood there watching Marcus, who was wearing a light green shirt and dark green tie, try to line up people to follow him in some dance. Damien was sitting in a corner with three other boys, and they all shook their heads no when Marcus said, "Come on." Then, I don't know why, but I looked at Lynn and asked, "Do you want to do that?" pointing at Marcus.

"Sure," Lynn said, and when the two of us got in the line, the DJ whistled into the mike. "You're in luck now, guys—here comes the fairer sex," which made Lynn and me look at each other and make faces because even though the DJ looked cool, he sounded like a jerk.

Mr. Wright was at the dance with his wife, who was very pretty and very pregnant, and he introduced me to her as his math tutor. "Hi, Tess," she said, like she knew exactly who I was, and I had to wonder if maybe she was the person who worked with the police department and had gotten the information for us.

Nothing much else happened at the dance itself. But the other very good thing that happened outside was that when Miranda and I were waiting out front for our "limo" to pick us up, Damien came and sat on the stairs with me. "Tell my brother I'll be back in a minute if he comes while I'm gone," Miranda said, heading back into school.

"I like your hair that way," Damien told me, his fingers going around his head in circles like my phony curls.

"I like yours that way too," I said, which was extremely stupid, since his hair is about an inch long and looked exactly like it looks every other day of the year.

Damien laughed and took off his jacket, and when he did that, I saw something that shocked me. A dark blue ink chain was drawn around his left wrist, and inside each loop of the chain there were dots: Damien was wearing the cheaters' tattoo bracelet.

"Did Luis draw that?" I asked, pointing to the phony bracelet.

Damien put his jacket behind us and sort of moved closer to me when he did that, so that his leg touched mine every time one of us moved. "Yeah," he said, leaning both elbows on the step behind us, where I couldn't see his wrist anymore.

"Why are you hiding it?" I asked.

"Because it's a wish bracelet," he said, smiling, "and maybe I don't want you to know my wish."

Miranda came back outside with James right then, and Luke showed up at that exact minute, jumped out of the car, and said, "At your service, ladies." Then he asked the boys if they needed a ride, and James said sure, but Damien said no thanks. So before I could find out anything more about Damien's wish, I had to stand up and say, "See you later," to him.

As I sat in the backseat of my limo staring out the window, I felt scared and confused. I knew I'd been really wrong about something, but there were a couple ways to be wrong about this, and I didn't know which it was. So while Miranda and James and Luke talked about the dance, I tried to figure it out. Either Damien was part of the cheating group and he just didn't get a good enough grade to be caught and I was wrong about him, or the bracelets had nothing to do with the cheating and I was wrong about that.

Luke must have gotten sick of opening doors, because when he stopped in front of my house, he just waited for me to get out. "Thanks a lot," I said, and waved good-bye to everyone.

I thought my parents were already asleep when I got home, so I took off my shoes, tiptoed into the kitchen, and sat down at the computer. About a second later my mother came downstairs in her pajamas and stood next to me.

"Have a good time?" she asked.

"Yeah," I said. "It was fun."

Mom leaned over and kissed my forehead before she went back to bed. "Remember to turn off all the lights down here when you go upstairs, please," she said.

Sammy was the only one on my buddy list who was online, and for the first time in five days I sent her an instant message.

"You okay?" I asked.

"Yeah," she said. "You home already?"

"Yeah," I wrote. "How come you didn't go?"

"It's been the worst week of my life," Sammy answered.

I didn't know what to say to that because 1) it had been a pretty lousy week for me, too, and Sammy's betraying me was the thing that started the lousiness; 2) one of the reasons the week was so awful for Sammy was that she has to raise everything, even bad things, to the fifth power, so a stupid coincidence—like three boys cheating and getting a hundred on the same test you really do get a hundred on—feels like a tragedy when it's not; and 3) her week could have been a whole lot worse if I hadn't gone into Ms. Balford's office and told what I did. But nobody knew about that, and I wasn't about to tell Sammy another secret yet, not even one about her.

I didn't write any of those things back to her, though; I didn't actually write anything at all.

"Did you wear the black dress?" Sammy asked.

"Yeah. Hey, did you ever notice the bracelets that Luis draws on people's wrists?"

"The wish bracelets?"

"Yeah. What's that about?"

"Alicia draws them too. She told me it was a Haitian thing—you wear it for seven days and then your wish will come true. Why?"

"Luis and Eddie and Richard were all wearing

them the day of the test. I thought they were connected to the cheating."

"Maybe they were wishing they didn't get caught," Sammy wrote back, and I wrote LOL even though I wasn't really laughing out loud and I knew Sammy wasn't laughing at all.

Sometimes when you're trying to figure out a math problem, you can do every single step correctly, but the answer still won't work, because you've found what's called an extraneous solution. That means that it's an extra answer that seems like it should be right, but for some reason—like say there's a zero in the denominator—it's completely wrong.

That's what had happened to me with the cheaters' bracelets. Even though they looked like they were part of the answer to how the boys had cheated, they were really just an extra answer that was completely wrong.

"How did they cheat then," I asked Sammy, "if

they didn't have the answers on their wrists?"

"It's not that hard to get the right answers when you've got the whole test beforehand," she wrote.

"True," I said.

Even though I couldn't see Sammy, I could feel how low she was. She just wrote, "I better get off now," and I just wrote, "Later."

Chapter 19
Asymptotes, Non-Euclidean Geometry, and Other Things I Didn't Learn Yet

I bet there isn't anything about asymptotes in our algebra book because people think the concept is too sexy for eighth graders.

Today Ms. Saltzman showed us the graph of a hyperbola that opened toward both sides of the paper, with two broken lines crossing right near it.

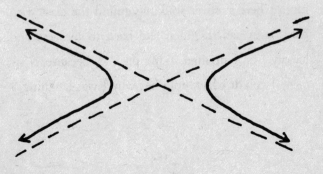

"It would be logical to think that if you plotted the complete graph of this hyperbola it would eventually cross these lines," Ms. Saltzman said. "But it never does." Her finger traced the broken lines as she said, "These are called *asymptotes*, which means that no matter how close the hyperbola gets, those lines never, ever touch it." Then she looked at her watch and said, "But we won't be studying asymptotes this year."

Right after that, while we were supposed to be doing pages 71–72 in our workbooks, Damien walked by my desk to return my art eraser. I put my hand out for it, but he didn't give it back; he just held the thing about a millimeter away from my opened palm until we both started to laugh.

"Would you like to tell us all what's so funny?" Ms. Saltzman called out from the other side of the room where she was walking around the class with her stamp pad. Damien slid back to his seat and luckily Ms. Saltzman didn't push it, because obviously I couldn't have told her why I was laughing. I couldn't have said that when Damien teased me, I understood how excited asymptotes get when those hyperbolas come so close.

Miranda thinks I'm naive about boys, but Miranda has no idea how I felt today when Damien didn't quite hand me the eraser.

When Ms. Saltzman stamped my workbook with a π and said, "Can you come by at three today?" she didn't sound angry at all, so I knew that coming after school didn't have anything to do with Damien and me laughing.

What it had to do with was the Math Counts competition in the spring. Ms. Saltzman was sitting at the long table by the windows with about fifteen folders filled with papers. She opened up one of the folders, gave me a brochure, and said, "If we do well, we get to go to the state level in Sacramento. Wouldn't that be cool?"

"Very," I said, taking the piece of paper she handed me, and then, even though she looked really busy, I sat down at the long table too.

Ms. Saltzman is the kind of teacher who hates to see you just sitting there. "Do me a favor," she said, handing me one of the folders and a hole puncher, "punch three holes in each paper and put them in the green binder." Then she got back to work, copying the number at the top of each of the papers into her grade book.

"How come you told us about asymptotes?" I asked after a while.

Ms. Saltzman stuck the first pile of papers into the first folder and put it on the floor by her feet. "I like to show you some of the fascinating things you have to look forward to," she said, and even though she couldn't *possibly* have meant what I was thinking, I felt embarrassed when she said that.

"If you continue studying math in college—and I hope you do," Ms. Saltzman said, "you're going to get into some concepts that are way out there."

"Like what?" I asked.

"Well, like non-Euclidean geometry," she said, opening the next folder and turning the page in her grade book. "That amazed me because, for one thing, in that system, parallel lines *do* meet."

"How can they?" I asked.

"It has to do with the earth not being flat," she said. Then she stopped working for a second to explain that if you draw parallel lines on the earth's surface, or on any other huge sphere, they will eventually cross at the poles. "It's only in Euclidean geometry that we behave as if all surfaces are flat," she said.

I punched a lot more holes while I thought about that.

Ms. Saltzman must have been thinking too, because after she closed one more folder and turned one more page in her grade book, she said, "It's all a matter of perspective. Like a lot of life, how we see a situation depends on how close we are to it. You know what I mean?"

"I do," I said. I was actually sort of shocked by what she said, because before that second I had thought I was the only person in the world who thought that way—that math could help you see everything else.

Ms. Saltzman didn't seem to think it was all that amazing, though. She just dumped another folder on the floor by her feet and picked up the next one.

"Did you ever think about Venn diagrams and friends?" I asked.

Ms. Saltzman stopped working for a minute and looked at me.

"Like, instead of showing what points two sets have in common, you could chart similarities and differences between people."

"I've never thought of it that way," she said, "but I have wondered if my sister and I were ever, or will ever, be on the same plane." Ms. Saltzman put one hand flat by her face and the other hand flat at her waist, which looked like she was about to do karate, but I knew each hand was supposed to be a two-dimensional plane. "We have no point or line in common; we share no opinion, idea, or feeling."

"If you drew a Venn diagram of your relationship," I said, "it would be an empty set."

"Exactly!" Ms. Saltzman said, lowering her hands. "Too bad I can't explain it to her that way—she'd think I was nuts."

I must have punched about fifty more papers, and Ms. Saltzman must have entered about fifty more grades before I said, "I didn't think I'd like algebra the first day of class."

"Why not?" she asked.

"Because you said algebra was the study of numbers that change. Like we couldn't use a number to represent our height, because that would be different in six months, so we should use the letter h, and p was for the price of our shoes, and s was the speed we could run. I hated that."

"Variables," Ms. Saltzman said. "What's wrong with variables?"

"They annoyed me."

Ms. Saltzman sort of laughed, but in a friendly way. "Why?"

I snapped open the rings on the green binder and started putting the papers in there. "Because math is supposed to be the place where something is either right or wrong, and when you know the answer it doesn't change," I said. "I always thought math was the one subject you could trust."

"Maybe that's the real lesson of algebra, honey—that everything changes."

I closed the green binder and leaned back in my chair. "Maybe that's why the infinity sign is like this," I said, making the loops of a sideways eight in the air with my finger and retracing it a bunch of times. "Always changing forever."

Ms. Saltzman looked up from her grading book, watched the movement of my finger, and nodded.

Then, while I rolled up the brochure she had given me, put it in my backpack, and stood up, Ms. Saltzman raised her arms in a big yawn.

"See you tomorrow," I said.

"Hey," Ms. Saltzman said, when I got to the door. "The first day of school, I bet you didn't know algebra would be so funny, did you?"

"What do you mean?" I asked.

"I mean whatever it was that you and Damien were laughing about today," she said. "But I have a feeling it wasn't directly related to mathematics."

"Yes, it was," I said, smiling. "Very directly." Then I waved and sort of ran out of there.

Chapter 20
Lines and Line Segments

When you know someone very well, you can pretty much tell how she's feeling about what you're saying even if she's just leaning her chin on her hand and staring at you. So I knew that my mother was angry when I told her I'd talked to Mr. Wright about Rob, and I knew that she was relieved when I said he'd learned that the police *had* done an investigation, and that they'd found "no sign of struggle." By the time I finished talking about the carbon monoxide poisoning Nina's body, I knew my mother didn't feel angry anymore. She felt really sad.

We were sitting at the kitchen table, supposedly eating dinner, but the pizza was still in the box, the lemonade was still in the pitcher, and my father was still at work.

"I was looking at the Citizen's Responsibilities poster on Mr. Wright's wall when I felt I had to tell him that we might know about a murder," I explained as my mother stared at her empty plate. "I felt like I needed some help," I said quietly.

"It wasn't like when I told Sammy and Miranda, because that was just wrong, and I'm sorry about that, Mom. That was awful, and I'm really, really sorry."

My mother sat back in her chair then, took an enormous breath, and when she let it out she said, "I spoke with Rob the other day."

My mother knows me very well too, so if she looked closely, she'd know that my first reaction was fear: I was scared that Rob had told her about me and Sammy going to his place.

"What'd you talk about?" I asked, watching my hands as I ripped a little skin off the cuticle around my thumbnail.

"I told him that I had set up my own small studio," Mom said, pointing toward our garage, "so I didn't need to use his anymore. He offered me his old pottery wheel," she said, "which was generous of him."

"Is that all?" I asked.

Mom shook her head. "I told him I wanted to know more about Nina's death. I told him that he had said some things the morning she'd died that had left me feeling very confused."

"You *said* that?" I asked, my head snapping up to look at Mom. "When you were *alone* with him in the studio?"

"Yes," my mother answered, reaching for the lemonade pitcher.

"Don't you think that was awfully dangerous?" I

asked. "I mean if there was even a one percent chance that Rob did it, there you were sitting alone with a murderer and asking him about it. Even *one-tenth* of one percent," I said, terrified for my mother even though I could see that she was perfectly fine.

"I don't figure out things mathematically like you do, honey," my mother said. "I tend to rely on my feelings. I felt safe with Rob, and I felt our friendship deserved the discussion."

I'd never wondered before if my mother was a brave person, but now, as I watched her pour lemonade into both our glasses, I thought that talking to a friend that way was incredibly courageous. When I took a sip of my drink, it was a little hard to swallow.

"What did he say?" I finally asked.

Mom stared at a spot in the middle of the table for a few seconds before she said, "Rob told me that they had stopped loving each other years ago.

He said that they lived very separate lives." Then my mother hesitated like she was deciding whether to tell me something very private, and I was really glad when she decided yes. "Rob was out with someone else that night," Mom said, "and he didn't return home until the morning. That's when he found Nina in the car."

My mother didn't even bother to wipe away the tears that were coming down her cheeks. She just sat there with a sad, wet face.

"Is that why Nina wanted to kill herself?" I asked. "Because they didn't love each other?"

"I don't know," Mom said. "There may have been other reasons."

Then my mother pulled a tissue from the pocket of her jeans. "There are a lot of ways to handle heartache," she told me. "Personally, I think Nina's choice was the worst."

"The very worst," I agreed as Mom wiped her eyes and blew her nose.

"Do you think Rob's glad she's dead?" I asked.

Mom sort of tilted her head back and forth—it was in between a yes and a no. "Rob said that for the rest of his life he'd regret that he wasn't home that night. But I do think he's relieved that the marriage is over." Mom tucked the tissue back into her pocket and said, "Rob told me he wished they had divorced—he said he thought they both would have been happier and maybe Nina would still be alive."

We were both quiet while Mom opened the box of pizza and put a slice on each of our plates. "I'm not sure you can understand this, honey," she said. "I'm sorry you even had to know about it."

"I can understand it," I said. "I can completely understand it. But still," I said as I picked the green peppers off my piece, "we can't be positive, can we?"

"Positive? No. But I believe in my heart that it's the truth. I honestly don't believe anyone could prove the theorem 'Rob killed Nina.'"

For some reason it made me feel extremely happy that my mother remembered what a theorem was, and I laughed when she said that.

Mom wiped some pizza sauce off the table, smiled at me, and shrugged.

Usually my father is the biggest talker in the family and so it's quieter when he's not at the dinner table. He's also the biggest eater, so it was funny that Mom and I ate nearly the whole pizza ourselves. There were only two pieces and a pile of green peppers left in the box when we stopped eating.

"What are you thinking?" she asked.

"You'll think it's weird," I said.

"Try me," my mother said, folding up her napkin and sitting back.

"Okay. I was thinking about the difference between lines and line segments," I said, which made my mother smile.

"I told you you'd think it was weird."

"Not at all," Mom said. "I'm always amazed at the way your mind works, but I don't find it weird. Tell me, please," she asked, "about lines and line segments, and why you're thinking about them now."

"Because of Nina's death," I said, and my mother sort of nodded like it made sense to her, although of course it didn't.

"In a line segment," I said, sliding my plate away, sticking my fingertip in a little puddle of lemonade and drawing on the table, "there's a beginning and an end, and you put dots here and here to represent those points."

"Got it," Mom said.

"But in a line," I explained, dipping my finger into my glass of lemonade and drawing a wet line with points at the ends, "you put arrows there, which means that the line continues past where we can see it.

"Theoretically," I said, "lines continue forever, and nobody can say if or where they end."

"How's that related to Nina's death?" my mother asked.

"It's just that I was wondering if, after you die, your life goes on like a line, beyond the point where we can see it."

"Or," my mother said, pointing to one of the wet dots I'd put at the end of the line segment, "if it all stops right here."

"Exactly."

"Okay, my turn to tell you something that *you* might think is weird," Mom said, sliding her own plate out of the way. "One day I went to visit your grandfather—I think it was about a month after Grandma died—and when I arrived, Grandpa was terribly frustrated because he couldn't find the car insurance papers. Before I could ask him where Grandma usually filed things, he got too upset and left the room."

My mother closed the pizza box and tucked in all the edges like she was putting it to bed. "Without exactly knowing I was going to do it, I stood alone in that room and I said, 'We need a little help here, Mom.'"

My mother's hands rested on the top of the pizza box like she wanted to warm them there, even though the box wasn't hot anymore. "I don't believe more than a minute passed before I walked over to Grandma's recipe books," she said, "opened up one that had an envelope sticking out of it, and stood there holding those car insurance papers."

"*That* is weird," I whispered.

"Really," Mom agreed.

"Why would insurance papers be in a recipe book?" I asked.

"Remember how Grandma always did too many things at once?" Mom asked, and even though she was smiling, she sounded like she could cry at any second. "Maybe one day while Grandma was opening the mail, she was also cooking and she decided she wanted to look up a recipe or something. Truthfully, I don't know, honey. But I do know that since that day," my mother said quietly, her finger touching the lemonade line with the arrows that pointed to forever, "I've believed this one is the correct answer to your question about whether there's some sort of life after death."

While Mom cleared the plates, I spread out my paper napkin and let the line and line segment seep right through it.

Chapter 21

Exponents

When Sammy apologizes, she does that to the fifth power too. She was standing on the stage in front of about three hundred people at the honors assembly when she told me she was sorry.

"I was asked to give this speech because I'm the Class Historian," she said, "so I feel a little bad that I'm going to be criticizing history, which is a subject I really do love."

They had already honored the students on all the athletic teams and academic teams and in the video club and dance club and cooking club, and actually anyone who did anything at all good during the entire semester. But even though nearly every person at school had gotten an honor, when Ms. Saltzman gave out a "Math Whiz" award and announced my name, it still felt wonderful when everyone clapped. I'm not sure *everyone* did, of course, but it seemed really loud in the auditorium when I walked up on the stage, and my hands and voice were shaking when I took the certificate and said, "Thanks."

I had just returned to my seat when Sammy started her speech, and I was sitting behind the two tallest boys in the school, so I had to lean over to see her. She was wearing a black headband and her long brown curls were all over the place behind it.

"The one thing that bothers me about history, though," Sammy said, "is that we never study anything about how friendship has changed through the ages. We read about how the workplace has changed and how family life is different and we read thousands of pages about wars and technology, but personally, I think friendship is the most important thing in middle school, and I wish we studied it more."

Sammy was speaking right into the microphone, which magnifies every single sound, so you could hear her take a deep breath before she said, "Even though I got A's in history my whole life, I almost flunked friendship this year. I broke my word to one of my best friends and I betrayed a confidence, and I want to take this time to apologize about that."

I leaned back so the tall boys' heads sort of protected me then, because when someone apologizes to you like that you have a lot of feelings that you don't want three hundred people to watch.

Sammy said that she only knew of one part of history that taught us about making up and forgiveness, and that was the Truth and Reconciliation Committee in South Africa, where former enemies came together to talk and listen to one another. Even though a lot of people in my school can be rude when someone speaks, this time the room was silent, so I knew Sammy's speech was pretty great. But personally, after the first few minutes, I couldn't really pay attention. I was just sitting there blinking back my tears and trying not to sniff or anything while Sammy raised our friendship to the fifth power.

Sammy's mother was standing in the back of the auditorium videotaping the speech, and when she turned to film the audience, I looked away so her camera wouldn't be able to find me.

Sammy's right about her mother's body being very skinny, without curves. But Sammy's wrong about the two of them not being the same in any other way, because after Sammy finished her speech, her mother put down her video camera, reached her arms over her head and applauded way up there. She hooted a little too, which I'm positive is exactly what Sammy would do if she had a kid and that kid gave a speech in front of the whole school. I'm positive she'd shout, "Yes, yes, yes, yes, yes!"

After Sammy walked off the stage, the dance brigade went up there and did this stomping, clapping thing without music that was cool, and the jazz band played two songs you could tell they hadn't practiced very much.

Then the assembly was finished and school was officially closed for vacation. We were all hanging out on the front lawn and some of the kids were shouting and hugging each other. When Sammy and I hugged, I whispered, "Thanks," into her ear.

Richard came right next to me and leaned down and for a second I had the ridiculous thought that he was about to hug me, too. But he didn't, of course. He just put his head close to mine and said, "I told on myself first, you know, before you even got back to school that day," which was his weird way of letting me know that he still thought he was > than me.

Damien didn't hug me either, but he said, "Hey, Math Whiz!" and stood next to me for a long time. He asked if I was going away over the school break and I said no, I'd be in town the whole time. Then I asked him if he was going away and he said no, and I said great. Then we both laughed for absolutely no reason.

Nobody noticed the fake tattoo that I'd drawn on the inside of my left ankle until Saturday afternoon when Miranda and Sammy were hanging out in my room.

Miranda was going to Chicago to visit her father for the holidays, so while Sammy and I sat on the floor, Miranda tried on every warm thing in my closet because it's always about two degrees below zero in Chicago.

"What does that mean?" Sammy asked, pointing

to the red design on my foot.

"Infinity," I said. Sammy looked like she was waiting for me to explain it a little more, so I drew ∞ in the air. "It goes on forever," I said as my finger looped around, "and everything always changes."

Miranda zipped up my green fleece jacket and turned toward us. "Was she nice?" she asked me.

I'd just told Miranda and Sammy about Mom's conversation with Rob, so I knew Miranda was asking about Nina. "She seemed really nice the one time I met her."

Miranda pulled my black wool hat over her ears. "It's so sad," she said.

"I still think Rob may have killed the cat, though," Sammy said, untying her shoes and kicking them off.

My bedroom is extremely small, so Miranda had to move a pile of sweaters onto the bed before she could sit on the floor with us. "Why would he do that?" she asked Sammy.

You could tell that Sammy was still trying to come up with a theory because she pulled off her socks, took a black pen from my desk, and studied her ankle for a while before she spoke.

"Maybe when Rob looked at Nina's pillow in the morning," she finally said, "he *did* see the cat there like he told your mother at first. So he picked it up and when he found Nina dead in the car, he put her beloved cat on her lap for comfort."

Miranda and I watched Sammy draw a line that curved down to her heel while we listened. "Or maybe after Rob opened the door of the car, the cat jumped in there," Sammy said, the point of her pen making small circles that were turning into a flower. "Then Rob went into the house and called the police, or maybe he called his girlfriend, or maybe he just sat down and cried," she said, a new idea coming with each petal. "In any case," Sammy decided, "when Rob went back out to the garage, the cat was dead too, because there was still enough carbon monoxide in the car to kill the little thing."

By the time Sammy finished talking, there was a

daisy growing from the stem on her heel, and I was thinking that her theory might actually be right.

"But even if something like that did happen," Miranda said, "Rob didn't mean to kill the cat then. He wouldn't do that."

"Can I draw a tattoo on you?" I asked Miranda, and when she took off her shoes and socks, I used my green pen to write $|m|$ on her ankle.

"What is that?" she asked.

"Absolute value," I said, feeling a little nervous that she wouldn't like it. "It's your symbol because you make everything positive."

Miranda bent her knee to hold her foot in her lap and then she nodded. "I'll take it with me to Chicago," she said.

"Do you have a math way of seeing me?" Sammy asked.

"I do," I admitted, and when Sammy scooted forward so her flowery foot was in my lap, I drew s^5 next to her daisy. "You raise things to the fifth power," I told her.

"I do?" Sammy asked, crossing her legs to see it better.

"At least," Miranda agreed.

They both sat looking at their symbols for a little while, and then without saying anything, we all straightened our legs at exactly the same time. Sitting on my bedroom floor, Sammy and Miranda and I formed a small circle, our three tattooed feet right in the center.

My heartfelt thanks to:

Annie Stine, who has edited every story of mine for many years, and who called me from the airport, with Chapter One in her hands, to say: Yes, absolutely yes.

My remarkably generous colleagues: Jane Meredith Adams, Annie Barrows, Karin Evans, Linda Peterson, Janis Cooke Newman, and Lesley Quinn.

My dear friends, who read and reread: Alice Abarbanel, Patty Blum, Nancy Cohen, Harriet Charney, Emma Haft, Jami Lichtman, Susan Sussman, Sonia Spindt, Agnes Wang, and Debra Weintraub.

My enthusiastic young readers: the eighth graders at Westlake Middle School, the ninth graders at the Lighthouse Charter School, the Book Club at Prospect Sierra School, and Sonia's Wednesday After-School Writing Group.

My agent, Steven Chudney, and my publisher, Virginia Duncan, both of whom make the business of writing a pleasure.

Dr. Robert Moses, whose work with The Algebra Project has informed and inspired me.

My beloved family: my father, Irv Lichtman, who took great pride in the fact that his girl liked calculus; my mother, Lenore Biltekoff Lichtman, who trusted me with this story; my children, Bekah and Lev Mandel, who read each chapter the moment I put it in their hands and gave me their criticism, praise, and love; and especially my husband, Jeffrey Mandel, first reader for more than thirty years.

And here's a preview of Tess's next
math-based mystery,

Do the Math:
The Writing on the Wall ...

Chapter 1

Patterns

"There was this tagger in Los Angeles," Sammy said, "who wrote coded messages about who was going to get murdered next. He knew that only one person in the city could figure out what he wrote, and that person *did* figure it out, but not until about six people were already dead." Sammy turned away from the graffiti wall to face Miranda and me. "From then on," she said, "the murders stopped."

Even though Sammy does know a million facts, she's so dramatic that it's always hard to know if what she's telling you is accurate or a major exaggeration.

"That's creepy," Miranda said.

We only had about five minutes before school started, and I wasn't really all that interested in checking out the graffiti Sammy was so excited about. But when she said, "What I'm thinking is that *this* could be a warning, too, and that the person who wrote it knew Tess would understand it," I looked at the numbers that were painted on the back wall of the church near our school.

There were about twenty bright green fours in the bottom corner, styled in a way that made it look like art—all different sizes and shapes—but still fours. They formed a messy circle, so I had to tilt my head from side to side to figure it out.

"*Do* you understand it?" Miranda asked as she handed me her denim jacket and took my white sweat-shirt. Miranda used to be smaller than Sammy and me, but ever since we got to eighth grade she's the tallest one—she's about two inches taller than me now, and I'm about two inches taller than Sammy. It doesn't really matter, though—we still always share our clothes.

"I think it's the Four Fours problem," I said, slipping on Miranda's jacket. "It's one of Ms. Saltzman's favorite things—she gives us these for warm-up at math team practice. You're supposed to be able to make nearly any number by using exactly four fours," I explained. "Like this one"—I pointed to $4 \times 4 - \frac{4}{4}$ — "would be the number fifteen."

"Clever," Miranda said.

"I *knew* you'd know," Sammy said. "What I'm thinking is that maybe this is like that guy in LA, and someone is telling you the next thing that Richard's going to do to you."

"Oh, come on," I said, picking my backpack up from the ground and tossing it over one shoulder. "*Richard* probably doesn't even know the next thing he's going to do to me."

Sammy shrugged. "I'm not saying for sure; I'm just saying *maybe*."

"Stop scaring her," Miranda said as the three of us headed toward school.

I had known that Richard would do something to get back at me for turning him in, but I thought it would be something big—maybe something so awful that I'd want to transfer out of Westlake. Instead, though, he was making me suffer by doing a lot of little mean things in the three weeks since we got back to school from winter break.

In a way, I thought as I opened my locker and saw the folded piece of paper that had been slipped through the slats on the locker door, that can be worse because then you're always waiting for the next bad thing to happen. Also, you have to spend your time wondering if he'll ever be finished.

I unfolded the note about five times before I got to the words that said, "Watch out, snitch." Miranda was standing next to me, and even though I was trying not to be scared, I could tell that she was—or maybe she just looked that way because she wasn't used to wearing glasses. She had gotten a pair over the break, and after reading the note she looked at me over the top of her glasses, not through the lenses. "You okay, Tess?" she asked, blinking her eyes as the bell rang.

"I'm okay," I said, shoving the stupid note into my pocket.

Ms. Saltzman had changed our seating at the beginning of the semester and most people complained, but I liked my new place in algebra class. There were seven tables in the room with four people sitting at each table, and one reason I liked the arrangement was that from my position at the table farthest back, I could see everyone else in the room. I could see Richard a lot more easily than he could see me.

"Mathematics is the study of patterns!" Ms. Saltzman announced as she walked around the room, her high heels clicking on the floor. Ms. Saltzman is single, and you can always tell if she has plans after work by what she's wearing. Sometimes she comes to school in slacks and T-shirts and no makeup, but this morning she was wearing a straight black skirt with a deep purple sweater, so you knew it was definitely a date night. Ms. Saltzman has brownish blond hair that always looks messy whether she dressed up or not, because that's her style.

Ms. Saltzman clicked to the front of the room and wrote the numbers 1, 6, 11, 16, 21, 26 . . . on the board. "It's pretty easy to find the twelfth number in this pattern," she said. "You'd just add five a few more times, right?" Then she turned toward us. "But what about the *thousandth*?" she asked, smiling, and you could just tell that patterns was one of the math concepts Ms. Saltzman was madly in love with.

A new girl named Lucia had come to Westlake this semester, and as I scanned the room I stopped to watch her for a while. Lucia wears silver rings on the first and ring fingers of both her hands, which I like a lot. She's about my height, but she looks like she weighs more than me—she's not fat, just curvier and strong looking. Lucia sits next to Marcus, and he's always doing things to try to get her attention. Anyone who's watching can see how much Marcus annoys Lucia because she leans way to her left to be as far away from him as she possibly can.

So I knew Lucia would be angry when, from my excellent new seat, I saw Marcus take a tiny pink canister out of the top of her open backpack and spray some perfume on the back of his hand. But I didn't know *how* angry she'd be, because I didn't know then that it wasn't perfume in that canister—it was pepper spray.

People have patterns, too, and I think the reason that nobody, not even Ms. Saltzman, paid any attention when Marcus started coughing was because of his pattern of doing things he thinks are funny, and phony coughing could easily be one of those things.

But it turned out those coughs were real, and about two seconds later my eyes started to itch and my lips began to sting. "You idiot!" Lucia shouted.

"I thought it was perfume!" Marcus said as he held the pink canister out to her. But before Lucia touched it, Ms. Saltzman grabbed the poison from Marcus, threw open the door to the classroom, and yelled, "Out!"

Then she raced to the window right next to me and shoved it open. When Ms. Saltzman turned around and saw that only Marcus had stood to leave the room, she looked at the coughing class like we were all morons. "I meant *everyone* out!" she shouted. "Stand up, for heaven's sake, and go out the side door to the yard." Banging open the second window, she yelled, "I do not want to hear one word on your way out there!"

That was more yelling than Ms. Saltzman had done the whole fall semester, so everyone did exactly what she said. We ran down the hall, out the side door, and onto the yard before anyone said a word. "You're a fool, man," Damien told Marcus, while we all stood in the cold, wet air.

Marcus was coughing and spitting on the ground in front of him, which of course gave Lynn the idea to fake a major coughing fit even though she sits at the table farthest away from Marcus and Lucia, so there was no way she could have been that irritated by one squirt of pepper spray. But Lynn's pattern is that she copies people; she does whatever someone else is doing. "It looked just like perfume," Marcus told Lynn, while they both stood there spitting on the blacktop.

Except for the area where Mr. Tran's cooking class planted a vegetable garden, the yard at Westlake looks like a huge parking lot with two basketball hoops at one end. You can borrow balls or jump ropes to use at lunchtime, but mostly people just hang out and talk. The graffiti wall is the back of the church that faces Twenty-seventh Street, and you can see it from the yard, but the only way to get there is to go through the garden and under the hole in the fence, and you're not allowed to do either of those things.

From too close behind me, I heard Richard's voice. "You'd go blind if someone squirted pepper spray directly in your eyes," he whispered. "Completely blind."

I could feel that he was smiling when he said that, but I didn't turn around to look. I just walked away fast, toward where Ms. Saltzman and Ms. Balford, the principal, were waving us over, and stood right next to Sammy.

Mr. Henley, the custodian, came walking across the playground with a pile of wet paper towels and told us to pat our eyes, noses, and lips. The air in Oakland in January is pretty much exactly like a wet paper towel anyway, but we did what Mr. Henley told us to do.

Marcus really isn't an idiot, so he never should have said, "I thought it was perfume" to Ms. Balford.

"Did you think it was *your* perfume, Marcus?" she snapped, which made him finally shut up.

"You are in the final semester of your final year of middle school, ladies and gentlemen," Ms. Balford said. "You are mature enough to know that if something is not yours, you do not touch it without asking permission from the owner. When I say you do not touch other students' property, I mean *anything*. Not someone else's desk, or backpack, or locker, or body. Is there any confusion about this?"

I was starting to get really cold and sort of wished I were wearing my own sweatshirt instead of Miranda's jacket, because a denim jacket does not actually keep you warm. I was holding my wet towel against my mouth, blowing warm air into it, and trying to blow a little of that air up the cuffs of the jacket when Ms. Balford said, "Take the towels away from your faces to answer me, please—is there any confusion about this?"

Everyone looked up and answered her question. No, we said, there was no confusion.

"I should mention," Ms. Balford added, "that Lucia had permission to bring this protective spray to school." Lucia was standing off to the side, not next to anyone, and Ms. Balford turned toward her to say, "Lucia, you did nothing wrong this morning."

I pulled my hands back as far as I could into

Miranda's sleeves while Ms. Balford went on about Lucia's mother having requested permission for her to carry the spray to school because her bus stop is in a neighborhood that doesn't feel safe. While everyone else was hugging themselves against the cold or bouncing up and down on their toes to try to get warm, Lucia stood perfectly still, and I wished Ms. Balford would please shut up and stop telling everyone Lucia's business.

So I was actually glad when Lynn interrupted with another fake coughing attack. Ms. Balford glanced in Lynn's direction but didn't fall for it. "One more thing before we go back inside," Ms. Balford said, swinging around and pointing to the back wall of the church. "This wall is also not your property."

About twice a year we get a lecture about the graffiti on that wall, and it was obvious why today was going to be lecture day.

You can't see the Four Fours problems from the yard, but you can see the huge new piece at the very top of the wall. Higher than anyone had ever painted before, someone had sprayed RISK IT! in red and black paint. Where the paint had dripped down, it looked bloody.

A lot of kids who aren't brave enough to spray paint their messages use regular marking pens to scribble where they can reach, but whoever wrote RISK IT! was plenty brave, because there was no way anyone could have sprayed that spot from the ground.

There's a sad-looking sunflower that's been at the bottom of the wall forever. The face in the center of the flower has eyes that look like they're about to cry and a mouth that dips down to one side. While I listened to Ms. Balford's lecture, I looked at that sad flower, its yellow, brown, and green paint all faded.

"I have asked the police to actively prosecute anyone caught writing or drawing on this wall," Ms. Balford warned, turning back to look at us. "If you borrow anyone else's property without permission, we will call it stealing; if you tag this wall, we will call it vandalism."

And what will you call it, I thought, hugging myself tighter, when someone writes mean notes and whispers threats about making you go blind? Will you ask the police to prosecute *him*?